MW01672871

Scholar by the Warsaw Fire:

A Short Story Anthology

Akiva Israel

Tate Publishing, LLC

"Scholar by the Warsaw Fire" by Akiva Israel

Published in the United States of America

by Tate Publishing, LLC

127 East Trade Center Terrace

Mustang, OK 73064

(888) 361–9473

ISBN: 1–5988631–7-7

CONTENTS

PART I

PART II

Selections

PART III

Part I

INTRODUCTORY MATERIAL CRITICAL TO THE READING

The short stories assembled for this anthology are actually selections, taken from novels I had written before the idea of bringing them together in this fashion had occurred to me. Being deliberately dispersed, they have been divided with an eye to the conscientious into numerous volumes, and with their presentation being serial, when one piece ends, the reader is prudent to keep in mind that the story has only been interrupted, not brought to resolution. This, however, does not apply either to the first or to the second entries in the collection, *Uriahkles* and *Marsailles*. It goes without saying that from the following remarks, one should expect the promise of further and future volumes, containing these stories.

Still, the endings of the first and second entries have been designed to reflect an overall kinship with their particular literary progeny, and are, therefore, products which produce specific emotional reactions.

These selections aren't adherent to traditional plot elements. By plot it is understood a causal sequence of events, which once employed, has the reader begin with exposition and/or narrative hook, information by which the story is made comprehensible. Additional material is introduced, thus complicating in its effect that it leads to the development of a major conflict for those characters either directly or indirectly involved in the story. The particular point at which this shift or catalyst, the cause for change in conflict for the charactership, occurs may also be referred to as rising action. This reaches climax, and hence this next stage for plot development is called climax, though rather unoriginally, I might add. Then, with the industry to have the conflict resolved exhausted, action falls. This latest series of events spirals into resolution, the few remaining fragments of development which thus end the story proper. This is the body into which the soul of the Muse has been thrown, how storytelling suffers the genius of creative intellect, that is, so to speak, how the technicality of plot structure works in mutual cooperation with the creativity of individual authorial tastes and talents. With respect to the architecture of *Scholar*, though, this accepted formula has changed.

In *Scholar*, the plot is merely an expression of a far more fundamental reality. It may begin at the end or at the beginning, as is commonly done in the written form of art, but as is the case with the industry of the ingenious, there is more than merely meets the untrained eye. Plot in *Scholar* has been made to reflect how all plots prior to its have not been designed to demonstrate their own futility. This point is complex, and I heartily refer the reader to "On the Wholeneficence" essay, for further explanation and elaboration.

The topic next for discussion is that of language. This will be brief.

Language in these selections is unlike anything the reader is likely to have encountered, during the course of their varied literary readings, since the twilight of High Renaissance Europe.

Refusing to yet reveal its name, it is a language built along classical lines. Ancient in purpose, it remains ageless in its ability to perform successfully the meaning for which it was chosen to exist, so long ago.

To learn the name for this function calls for the reading of the book. As was the case with the old Greek practitioners, it is rebellious to a monotonous tense for the verbs it has been called upon to employ. This unique effect is imperative for its design. See "The Representation of Time" essay for additional elucidation.

When necessity and creativity were mutual, if not practically indistinguishable, for the practice and the preservation of the English language, during the reign of Queen Elizabeth I, it was common for writers, the minds of the Muse, to redefine words as they saw right fit, coining fresh species thereof, with adamant, abundant fervor. I follow the tradition. It is to be noted that their definitions and/or redefinitions are established contextually.

Thematically, *Scholar* is traditional but not to current conventions in the field, which is to say that false filth for a book flung face-first into the public feast for fickle consumption. It is inconvenient to satisfy conventions established in the name of mediocrity by sacrificing the deathless in genius; it is a blessing to show an audience, starved for freedom from filth and falseness, the face of the fear, which made that corrupted construction of current literary convention seem fruitful and faithful to the individual ideals of artistic integrity and ingenuity. The starvation for such food makes the creative forgers of words in part farmers, and if the allusion is continued, famines have too often framed the canvas of those desperately referenced bestseller lists in the popular papers of the printing press, which seek audience with the artistic and the assemblies in admiration of the artists.

The world in which *Scholar* lives is infinitely paradoxical, and ceaselessly fettered to the ironic. At the end of this, I call into service the words of Mr. Kippelstein, who described the situation hauntingly at its best, "Gentlemen, I will give you the universe, but you will have to find God for yourself."

The Idea of Angstrophy: A New Genre

In order to better explain this new genre, I have taken the liberty of snatching a page from someone's notebook; but being precise, I've also resorted to changing some of his tone and beliefs so that they may be a little less incomprehensible, shorten the paradoxical but all the while running the risk of making it all the more unattainable.

This idea should've been written down a long time ago, and it was; but being forgotten, its creation is then more like remembering the face of an old friend whom we haven't seen for quite a while.

Struggle and the struggle against struggling are not enough. The world loves a good fight, but misunderstanding what it is about is no less tempting, and nor is it any less terrible than losing. For me, Rightness dictates that there's no difference between some drunk hitting another drunk's head over with a beer bottle in your local tavern, than there is with a scholar arguing the most detailed points of ancient philosophy and correlating it with the most pressing contemporary issues in the strongest nations' most prestigious universities. No difference. Don't get me wrong, though. My concern is quite simple.

The ancient minds of creativity, especially those of Greece and the Near East, knew how to draw certain distinctions, yet never losing an eye to simplicity while securing an ear to subtlety, sacrificing only the illusory. The distinctions they drew weren't butcheries, but intricately woven tapestries of painstaking labour. It is this that made them fortunate and adopted, lonely with truth, young progeny—children of the sublime.

There's no room for escapism in creativity, only reality as seen through genius: yet another notion which hasn't fared well either. It's all about longing but not the kind that's most associated with what is now commonly referred to as sensible, practical, or even reasonable, no. These words have been misunderstood, a carnage of what they had once been when the creative genius didn't butcher himself, his hand forced by the temperately mad to inflict upon himself the wounds of those who have now been lost.

Creativity and reality are intimately connected, like death and sleep, or better yet, death and wisdom.

There was a time when the creative act was seen as divine. It was a reality of such grace and dignity that more than memory seems to allow men such as Odysseus saw in it the face of God, staring at him quietly. Given their earthly, very much commonplace, no-nonsense occupations, the Ithacan would, for example, upon being made the judge of whom would have to be slaughtered, of who's disposable, either it's a priest or a minstrel, would confidently declare that the minstrel, being a direct link with the divine, could not be touched, not a single hair was to be ruffled. Having spoken in this vein, he was quick to draw his sword, slaying the priest instantly. The priest was a man of nobility, whose flesh was conscious of privilege and prestige, fortune being a constant mistress in his fate's night-time bedchamber. To say it simply, without having to say it simpler, the man of the Gods was, usually, an aristocrat who knew the tortuously established ins-and-outs of his kingdom's political discourse, a pluralistic agency, being it was not uncommon for his mind to think thoughts of foreign interest, all of which were, unsurprisingly, quite domestic to the person rather than to the body sat atop the throne—so that then he was fully capable of serving the state and serving it well. The minstrel, on the other hand, was a simple, impoverished wanderer, who sang songs in his singsong voice, telling old tales, reminding his audience of what it all was about. He wasn't a noble, but what service he rendered was the noblest thing we may yet begin to imagine, not leaving one corner of either truth or nature untouched. His was, then, a singular consciousness, with such wholeness, that today it is hard for the inhabitants of the present to fully appreciate the power of an act of creation, as by words, of which, again, wasn't entirely deprived in the past.

To exert harmony on language, in a creative way, ennobles so as to empower the one to do readily, what is normally done reluctantly. Harmony allows for the comprehension of nature and of our own natures by doing nothing more or less than using words, our words, to communicate, calculate and generate the world in which we live, and of which we aren't necessarily fully conscious. Do not allow forgetfulness to have the fact that tells us that in Genesis, God created the world not with violent deeds, as in the ancient mythologies, but by simply putting words into sentences, and speaking them aloud. The near unspeakable feats of the savage imagination are denied, and thus we see him not as the conqueror-creator, but, indeed, as the solitary artist, which alone, inhabits creatively his lonely universe: a "wandering" entity of eternity. We mustn't forget either that God just might turn out to be nothing more or less than a literary character, an invention that became an act of creation. I wouldn't put it passed possibility, but then again, whatever is.

True art doesn't evoke creation; it is itself an act of creation that becomes conscious, being and becoming aware of what there is to be recognized. This is an aspect of art, not its nature.

There was a time when words weren't merely negligible utterances, used and abused merchandise, some returnable item that could've been ignored; a minor inconvenience to be swept quickly underneath the rug of objective incredulity. Words are now mere shadows devoured by that darkness which the evening of history brings, museum pieces to be talked about behind closed doors, meaning little for a world hungry for such food. They are like certain people whom you might've met up at school, lonely curiosities. Stranger individuals, who always had the ability to draw the mind closer to something, and yet for petty reasons, excuses really—be they embarrassment or plain discouragement from false friends—fill the list out as you have to; they were never approached. And consequently a person from whom one might have learned so much is lost, an opportunity of such worth, taken away from one forever.

Suddenness is fond of silence. Perhaps you've experienced what I am attempting to explain for yourself, so when I write about how certain events in nature are so immediate and living, that they go unnoticed, isn't registered at all by consciousness, the forces of the faculties in refusal, or, imaginably, deprived of means by which to have registered what has happened at all, it'll strike you as seeing something quite familiar due to its unmistakable strangeness, which experienced once, imprints deeply a scar into the spirit of the times. It's during times such as these when one realises the opportunity, which has been lost, the door through which one could've entered but is now locked; the key never to be found again. The moment of realization sudden like the point at which one awakes from sleep, the usual silence escorting the emotion no different than inaudible apparitions haunting pastures in the countryside.

It's a matter of desire, that lingering longing born when one sees what there is to be seen, the willingness to allow a word, the seed of creation, this infinite powerhouse of raw reality at its finest, simplest, and most extraordinary, to grow into a giant. Now it's an immense imposition, doing little for nobody.

To discover all over again the true nature of words is where angstrophy begins; it's when the ice-axe falls upon the sea frozen deep inside you, which by its more proper name is called consciousness.

That is the angstrographical, how it begins: immediate and distressing and real, an old friend.

On the Wholeneficence

A plot is usually defined as the way in which the events in a drama or some other narrative work have been arranged. Its idea lies in each event being the seed from which grows the tree on whose branches are hung the causes that lead to what follows next, all the while the tree is firmly rooted in the ground of conflict. One has a protagonist and an antagonist in this structure, with accompanying ornaments such as exposition.

To begin with, the technique of the wholeneficence lies in each event being the ground from which a mountain rises, has its home, around which conflict is merely so many rivers, brooks, crooks and other such like tributaries meander. The actual mountain is composed of two elements; these being iconicality and reaphorism, with the latter signifying the underlining struggle for the adversative untagonist, and the former the untagonist proper. If there are any lingering questions concerning the definitions of these two terms, one merely has to reference their etymology to know why they are as they are.

The Representation of Time

Time is an inconstant fire, a Northern Star of uncertainty in which all burns with the precision of a dream. The written form of angstrographical art isn't concerned with evoking its subject, has no business with it at all.

To achieve this aim, the angstropher has all but done away with the staleness of a monotonous tense. It was a common practice for the Greek writers of antiquity to keep switching the time of events, making menace with the monotony of a stale narrative. This was their way of making a scene immediate, striking the reader with a sudden surge of solicitude, snapping him out of the sleepy spell of resignation at the fact that what he is reading has already happened, and though it could have happened some other way, what he reads now is basically fate's fine print, a perpetual publication not to be changed. To put terror into the tense was their way of setting the scene in accordance with the lively, so as to stir in the reader the certain sense of the story being alive, alerting him to how abruptly awareness could be changed, and casting what he's reading into a new light; it's happening now, and so what may happen is up for grabs, a chance of escape. These two keys secured, the door to reality is unlocked. To present the action as having already happened, in the past, and then recasting it as something that is happening now, in the present, is imperative in the efficaciousness and consciousness of angstrographical art. But there is more.

Terrorizing the tense is not merely a means of evoking the story; it's a way of actually creating its reality, of setting the stage on which such action may take place, to make it possible. Abraham's offering of Isaac to God is a testament to his faithfulness, as much as it is to his faith, so too is the sacrifice of time a testament to steadiness, as much as it is to constancy. This drama, however, is to be reenacted in the reader, each character his own being, the decision entirely his own in an otherwise characterless world. The actual angel, however, whom has been charged to stop the sacrificial hand from making the lethal incision, is that state in the reader that makes it possible for him to understand, really and truly, the subtle, ironic, and paradoxical nature of the angstrographical.[1]

[1] I shall end with this footnote: there are three central characters as there are three principal tenses.

PRONUNCIATION KEY

~

Uriakles (yoo'rie ´ah'kleez)
Neptonius Gaius Tiberius (nehp'tohn'ee'uhs, gie'uhs, tie'beer'ee'uhs)
Julia Daphrodite Flavius (dah'frah'die'tee, flah'vee'uhs)
Dericles (dehr'ah'klees)
Lucius (loo'shehs)
Antonius (an'tohn'ee'uhs)
Lucidriclesius (loo'si'drah'klee'see'uhs)
Eurythikles (yoo'rith'ah'kleez)
Doulpsyche (dool'sie'kee)
Sharhanim (shar'hah'neem)
Marsailles (mar'sie)
Manasseh (mah'nah'sah)
Shoach (shoh'akh)
Tolocusah (tuh'luh'coo'sah)
Maracelsus (mar'ah'sel'ses)
Nazarich Shlomowitz (nah'zehr'rik, shloh'moh'witz)
Akeiden (ah'kie'den)
Hesch (heh'sh)
Disiconoclastacy (dis'eye'cahn'noh'clahs'tah'see)
Messianic Extremecy (ex'treh'mah'see)
Solicicence (sah'lih'sah'sehns)
Occultastrophe (oh'cul'tahs'truh'fee)
Ucarnacity (oo'kar'nah'sah'tee)
Inprincilency (in'prin'suh'lehn'see)
The Agisony (ah'gihs-ah'ee)
Angstrophy (äõs'truh'fee)

PART II
Selections

The Syntax of Uriahkles

I shall build thee an awful sacrifice
—Whereby old Abram hopes whilst I had none.

DOULPSYCHE the elder

Imperfect silence mingles with mangled hands, and the day is already set apart from its counterpart, night, but nature yet remains indifferent to the disturbing spectacle. The wind whips up against his face, the mind is devoid of thought, his hands and eyes appear rebellious to the world of movement and living things in general; he is alone, but not a stranger to himself. He sees the sun, but the item of mortality, in whom we may find a steady faculty, is not blind to the blindness that is about him.

When light rose that morning the sun did not seem shy to Uriahkles, but for him this great miracle is a great monster, the point at which this became so is now insubstantial: like a dream. The sun is death's harbinger now; he is even, perhaps, its hunter. This Roman, Uriahkles, is a survivor and, being precise, he is a soldier who has been orphaned by the proud progeny of Mars; he has been left for dead by the legion for which he had fought. He is a child of accident, who owes heavily to the accidental. Purpose was when indoctrination was an intellectual intoxication, a drug for which he had the strongest craving, and the sincerest respect. This is passed him, some uncertain Siren prison from which he has escaped, by escaping to yet another inevitable indubitable penitentiary.

The vultures, they whose chief virtue is patience, have feasted hungrily. The bones are strewn indiscriminately across the plain, with marks bearing their uncanny precision. The transformation is tragic, with its nature being defined by no uncertain qualities—the memory of strange desires, with the conscious disgust of grotesque deeds: a ubiquitous ugliness. The desire to defend by death their dignity, the passion born of privilege for the preservation of principality, both of which became greater with the addition of the longing for liberty, which is for the pursuit of laziness insofar as the Romans are concerned, such distant honours, have been estranged because of the strangeness of what has now happened. The faces of intimate friends and imperturbable compatriots cannot be of whichever word any uglier or more explicitly described than as a waste-heap, its content: violated bones accompanied by heavily bloodied incandescent armour. This, too, is food for memory, which also waits hungrily for time to hunt down its prey, an unsuspecting victim. The heart is intoxicated with fear, but definite terror has, so far, been unable to assume residence upon the seat of passion, but silence is the music of fate from which none have escaped, save only Uriahkles. There is no expectation, trivial or otherwise, in contradiction to this once established truth to be found lurking in the soldier's mazy meandering mind. He is publicly alone, not to be further delusion by that great temptress, which is called hope, never again.

The desert is a hostage to silence, but the dead, as destroyed as they are, are free from any such captor.

Lifting himself up from off the ground, he prepares to embark upon a future established by uncertainty, but desire is certain to follow him and in more ways than one.

The lonely soldier, a solitary now, wanders for quite some time, until the sun has run its course when, finally, he decides to ready himself for rest. No food has his mouth known, nor water or hope have been welcomed to his faculty, which is now weakening steadily. There is a mountain not far from where he is now, and so he goes to it, his shadow like a ghost dragging him in his desire. Unfortunately, but unavoidably, nothing of utility does come out of it, except hard stones for pillows, but then again, this he had already had.

Closing his eyes, quieting the mind, he is embraced by a sudden sleep, which is discourteous. Time smiles at him, but underneath these facial courtesies the solitary's mind finds only starving crocodiles, the smiling murderers of nature.

Uriahkles regains consciousness with the rising of the sun; the speed at which this comes to pass is reminiscent of deep drunkenness, incandescent depravity to which weakened sense remains ignorant. Finding himself awakened, he sees that he has punctuated the ground, on which he slept, with his nightlong twisting and turning—the sandy labyrinth of his various movements do not disturb him. It is unexceptional.

He sits still, and refuses to move. He continues in this manner for quite a while, remaining immobile, until finally, the darkness of evening has fallen upon him. Having freed himself from this posture, he sets out at once to explore further the expanse; consequently journeying deeper into darkness.

There is no denying the dread fact that his constitution has significantly worsened. The face is gaunt. The fingernails have grown excessively, as have their counterparts, with a few being only freshly broken. The blisters are ubiquitous; their presence is equalled only by the dryness of the skin, which is desperately conspicuous.

He finds in his frenzy a few wild fruits; no doubt, they are clear indicators of passing treasure caravans. His only choice is to make a choice, and thus he consumes, only to be consumed in turn—He vomits violently, until he begins to throw up blood, which mixes disturbingly with pale moonlight. This dismal disgrace lasts for an hour, and continues inconstantly throughout the remainder of the night.

Waking up the following morning pain greets him faithfully. The stench that encircles his person staggers his temperate disposition, yet there are no diatribes. His lips are burnt, and the ache of the teeth is slowly beginning to become unavoidable. Vision has the weary precision of a dream, and all else is consigned to a declining mind. He is unable to move, but from this time onwards his maladies begin to spread, spreading to his whole constitution, and his appalling sufferings have now begun to take a variety of forms. Rain came, but each tear heaven weeps peels proportionately layers from off the flesh. He has a raging fever, which even in sleep continued to pang him, with each individual mediocre dream born therein a frightfully tortured vision of such inconceivable agony. That same recurring dream dreamt during the day, his survival in absolute sufferance, is evolving into greater evil. It is increasingly becoming a sinister summons to continual screaming, a white wolf howling at his own arrival to pain by moonless night. The dreams haunting his mind are relentless, like demons, those thick-hatred hearted knights, obsessed beyond madness with their pursuit of their tortured punishment of sinners down in deep dungeons, the deepest of still deeper hell, or ghosts, thin-conscious controlled guardians, out in the countryside to avenge wrongs not yet corrected by flesh-frenzied judges, are inescapable, uncontrollably ingenious resurrections of the nightmare festering in the flesh whilst awake. An intolerable itching of the whole skin subtracted much requisite rest from him. The vomiting of blood was not uncommon. Insufferable sensations of starvation steadily persisted. The intestines suffered ceaselessly consequently, with his stomach now assuming a tumourous disposition. Inflammation of the abdomen and reoccurring flashbacks of active combat, which he had witnessed during the siege, haunts him throughout the night. And so the agony inconceivable to days lived during the flesh of innocence worsens, with his engendering worms, in addition to his having growing difficulty in breathing. The beauty of life was the brevity of simplicity, but he had already known this. Sickness of his soul does cause much anguish and whispering, the unchecked sufferings of the constitution are great, but added together, they fuse into a terrible forgetfulness, a monstrous industry of turning one's gaze towards the awful liberation of the demonic. The reality to which we affix dread realisation is fast approaching midnight: reckoning or rioting is about to ensue; there can be no reconciliation between the two. Perhaps, he shall not discriminate between them.

The winds are blowing softly, as there is much whispering occupying his mind, which, controlled in nature, has still that unease he has seen when seas are whispering gently; until such a time when the storm-poised womb of Neptune gives birth to the monsters of the abyss, stimulating in their wake just as much fear as mortality.

Distant childhood is rarely distant from present adulthood. Present nature is outstripped by old memories, which, so far, had not been stronger than their counterpart. Rebelled, replaced and reformed, his memory abandons reading the grand book of the world in order to peruse contemplation in the infinite distance of darkened space, this being that golden city, curious childhood, whose light has long since ceased to burn.

The night had run its course, and soon morning came, its beauty was this time crowned with fog, the curtains behind which a silent dream-drama was about to unravel in Uriahkles' mind.

He sees old things made new by remembering them. The innocence of being a child of curiosity gave way to the experience of his having become an orphan of incuriosity.

The army seems so far away now. Remembrance, this indefinite faculty, appears to be cradled not by an event in his biographical history, but by a daring, audacious, even fantastic episode which is solely tenured by the imagination. His is now an autobiographical notation which, however perspicuous, catches dictation from the latter faculty, rather than its rival, which is a different form of creativity in disguise.

The first day came like a lazy miracle; the previous lifestyle he had known was gone, but not dead. Even then he recalled a quiet hunger for home, this somewhat irritating sense of a shared history of suffering and longing which the whole world appeared to keep silent about;

unable, it seemed, to confess the truth for which it had been created.

The traditional course of basic training was monotonous, nullifying and invigorating, as he had thought it would be. The voice became instrumental to its cause: shouts, screams, and speeches all constituted, all came to create–so he contended–an individual ideological entity of which he knew nothing, but for which he would be proud to forfeit his life.

The naked monotony, from which he shall emerge clothed in obedience and dogma, is beginning to understand his intemperate character; it has begun to read him like a book, swallowing him up like one swallows food or water. The instruments he uses are precise; the oaths of loyalty are sworn. The woodened, now metallic, symbolism to which he has pledged his allegiance saturates him like marriage vows taken by idolatrous lovers or flagrant miscarriages of justice committed by crafty criminals. He has friends; he met them—he has forgotten the details. Their names are Dericles, Lucius, and Antonius. If one were to contrive a scenario, considering the fact that the presence of particular instruments for want of being at one's disposal is met, continuing thus with the intention, in which certain distinctions are denounced so as to delineate from these labours a fitting frame of reference, they are, these former friends of his, in like manner to nature's four seasons: Dericles the winter of the heart, a cold but obedient soldier; Lucius the summer of the memory, a warm, workable, and inviting cartographer, whose precision of art complements the fragile perfection of his odd social habits, the details of which we need not introduce; Antonius the autumn of folly, engaging, exciting and never sober but always god-intoxicated, Bacchus' religion was his pastime during his prime, like it was for many others'; and Uriahkles, he fancies himself the spring of intellect, an equilibrium to the chaos.

He remembers, as so they say, the good and the bad, but the precise characteristics of the people, places and things he has experienced have now been lost, stolen by sickness, sadness and time, which itself may be the illness of which he spoke in earlier years.

The strange session, this reverend remembrance! It is a massacred body spitted upon the pike, dashed to pieces, a conquest in time through which meaning and madness have ground. Desire denied, purpose unto accident thus impressed pang him further, as so to tell of small pleasures now forever lost. He will admit to the worse how the desire to remember, and remember well, burns deep within him: basic training, inspirational hand gestures, anthems, the initial implements issued and active combat done, spiral about his being; these disturbances cause him to look back as the hungry hatred greets redemption nigh. The words of a personal proverb ring more true now than they did before, "Tribute of the tribute through violent swing into chaos struck strikes fast temperate things."

His friends have blurred into a single image or frame or representation; to reason most clear there is no Dericles, Lucius or Antonius, but one mere being–so he contends–which he calls Lucidriclesius.

He remembers his parents, they who are now mourning him. He has no siblings, or relatives and the grandparents through both bloodlines did not live to witness his birth. His friends from the army days have long been digested; the vultures are now waiting for him to follow in their abhorrent fates. They could be seen hovering high overhead, occasionally. No wife, no children; he has himself. Young Uriahkles, the body is abused by exhaustion and starvation, the mind is filled with anger, hopelessness—but the soul is haunted by the ghosts of the past.

He grew up in a villa, a rather big villa, he thinks. The field was graced with figs, apple trees, wheat, barley, corn, fallen leaves from the old tree, servants occupied in their various duties; there's a giant arch by the gates. The baskets are full with the fruits garnered during the harvest; a goodly meal is surely to greet him when darkness falls that evening. He remembers seeing white stallions galloping across the cornfields, a neighbouring river empties its waters into a larger stream; this is to be done until the gentle cycle is possessed of the promise of time's continual fire.

His father's name is Neptonius Gaius Tiberius. He is a gentleman of property who has fought in many of the great campaigns of the empire; he is now retired, a farmer with a predisposition for book learning and logical argument. His mother is the golden-haired Julia Daphrodite Flavius, a gracious hostess sought-after for her excellence in herbal remedies, horticulture and harp playing, which is always accompanied by her singsong voice. Her hymns are an eloquent testament to the family's idyllic but noble lifestyle. He was, he remembers, kind and, yes, friendly to the servants, as are his parents; they all adore the little master, very much. The gymnasium does him honour and is in turn honoured by his presence. The gods have blessed him with these memories, he thinks.

"Come, Uriahkles, come," says his father; "hurry now, or else you'll be late. We cannot have that from you." The kind and familiar voice is certainly a memory, but the thought of it being as much rings not only untrue, but also hollow and unfamiliar. The first word spoken was "*Mousa*." It is Greek. It is, specifically, the title that designates the daughter-goddesses of Mnemosyne, the deity representative of memory or, rather, its personification in the ancient Greek pagan religion, all of whom are better known as Muses, or the Reminders: for that is a translation of their Greek appellation. He has been taught that they chant hymns on sacred mountains, inspiring great men of genius, reminding them–quite literally–of their god-invested personalities, along with its serious potency and heavy duty. His parents thanked the Olympians many times for giving them their first and only son: their only child. The inviting flagrance of burnt incense incites the sense, but this too is fictitious.

His father stirs his sleepy son, and tells him not to stray far today, because they are going to go soon.

"Worry not, father, I shan't stray far to-day: looking is all," his son replies.

The boy is on his way to the stadium, where he soon sees great beasts engaging in savage struggles with armoured gladiators. The clamour of the crowds echo, rising from the stadium until the roar of the spectators appears to build itself into a tower with its top in the topmost Olympus. The lions are occasionally disturbed rather than distracted by the cacophony, Uriahkles notices. In Rome, he discovers, it is the enduring impulse to see the spilling of brave human blood; as for cowards and martyrs, this makes but pastime for the "imperturbable audience," as Uriahkles is for want of calling them.

These great cathedrals of Death are ubiquitous all throughout the empire. The spectacles are sudden in pleasure, savage in nature, but demonically elegant in their simplicity. Uriahkles sees them in this way, and grows to distrust them before the eclipse of adolescence

The Circus Maximus, there the speed is swift, he observes, as a silent wind is in the night. The violent breezes leave the leaves to uncertainty, just as the serene dreams of the dreamer are met by a moment's wake. This, too, is random in nature, so he thinks. The moment of clash is set, and the seasoned gladiator is struck, whereupon he falls from his stallion. Pain greets him with dust and shadows. There's applause, too. The unruly crowds clamour their overtures to the game's end, and the awards are thus distributed. Long into the night, if not indeed all night long, he thought about the gladiatorial games, lying quietly still on the bed of his mind, more so than on its counterpart. Though consumed in his contemplations, he neither dreams nor thinks about the games but *feels* them alive in him, and this, more than anything else, disturbs the mind. The extent to which this is thus may only find expression when conflagrations feed off the appropriate woods, as so to inflict upon the original landscape a novel self. He decides to abandon them, much to the pleasure of his mother, and to the annoyance of his father. Still, they accept his decision, and the matter is not to be discussed any further.

"War is the more ingenious!" Uriahkles exclaims. The frame of thought required to quiet the mind, and the requisite endurance equally called upon to control the pains and convulsions of the constitution were, to say the least, spectacular. Uriahkles imposed upon himself such strength in order to speak thus.

No longer a soldier with sword, the short thrusting gladius, but desolated, impoverished, a solitary wandering in the desert; he suddenly sheds his armour, clawing at it with his hands, a lion ripping at the carcass until from its flesh its bones are hacked, the fresh flesh consumed with fire in the eyes, swallowed impatiently. Exerting a profound endurance in his limbs, he beats his shield with his sword, until the former is cracked and rendered crippled of its purpose. These remains he throws into the waters of a nearby stream that seem to break off into yet more streams leading to a river. A mirage.

He does not tear the identity emblems of his garb, all of which mark him as Roman and a soldier.

It appears that his only goal now is to feed maggots and excel their wild growth to flesh-eating worms.

The kitchen, he recalls something interesting about the kitchen, the effort to remember disrupting the pain. This is, however, a tyrant-thought or, rather, a ghost haunting his mental processes, oppressing its operations. The spark is about to be extinguished, not to be rekindled ever again. The Fates–he believes–have finished with his fabric, the violent act of separation between his body and soul is now therefore the promise for which he has been assigned. The sensation is of an eccentric nature, he argues. Hands, mangled hands appear to be lifting him up from off the ground. Thus does death come to him, but it is too late.

~

Barely conscious of his environment, he is as if he were dreaming. He hears men arguing.

"Is he awake yet?" inquires a strange but imposing voice.

To which an answer leaps in the air, calm but worried in its tone: "Sir, the reoccupation of the faculties, especially with regard to consciousness, cannot be hurried, at least not without profound injury. Give him, I pray you, until the ascent of the chariot to wake him, that he may be cogent, in full possession of his faculties and ready to receive your questions. You do not wish to invite, certainly, a risk which may deposit dubious information into the hands of Rome, as so to strengthen the prospects for our enemies. For were I to wake him now, before the youth has made a full and natural recovery, his thought and the understanding are surely to espouse precepts induced not by reason, when she is tenured to her true self, but by apprehensions made nauseous due to an incapacious, though passing, disposition. Health. This, as I have consistently contended, shall come to pass, and it shall pass by the ascent of the chariot. His Majesty has commissioned my services, has charged me with the welfare of the sons who enable her to wage warfare, and I intend to honour the Emperor by committing myself to prudence, rather than to recklessness. It is no surprise, therefore, that when I am called upon to submit my testimony before the Imperial Throne, I am expected to present a history completely in harmony with His Majesty's expectations, as well as a register chronicling all those agents which assisted thus, as so to have secured, with Athena's counsel, the territorial integrity of the Realm.

"This is, General, the will of Caesar."

The reply over, the final decision is pronounced, "Then be it so."

He is alone again, for it appears that the officers have taken their leave of him.

Dreams come, and in no short succession, where once memories had occupied hungrily, the desire to remember is soon triumphant against them, however. He wakes to find himself in a tent, overlooking a familiar plain.

Dawn.

"Good morning, Uriahkles," greets the doctor. Not allowing for a response, he continues, "You have been rescued by a centurion and returned to camp. I have reintroduced health to your body by reason of rest and herbal arts, and in twenty-four hours you are expected to resume your duties to Rome. The war appears inevitable now.

"I do not want you to waste precious strength in speaking to me, especially when there is no need to continue this conversation. Please understand that were it up to me, I would send you to see your mother and father right away. Yes, they've been told as well as all of Rome. The Emperor has fashioned your name into a symbol of Roman strength, Caesar's emblem of indestructibility, but in brief His Majesty has made you into an ambassador of Rome's divine right to rule over all other peoples. So it is imperative to keep quiet about the details concerning your survival. It is held that—" the doctor is interrupted by an intruding officer.

"Ah, there's the strength of Rome!" he exclaims.

"Good morning, General," says the doctor.

"Yes, morning, Doctor. So tell me, good Uriahkles, are you ready to resume your duties to Rome?" asks the General.

To which Uriahkles lowers his head. He then says, with his head rising, "I am."

"Excellent, son, excellent," says the general, impressed as he is by the man, he nonetheless attempts to check his sense of veneration, and continues, "I shall see you later this evening for dinner. We are going to hold a lavish banquet in your honour, soldier." This said, he passes a glimpse at the physician, for whom he doesn't care particularly, and then redirects his gaze towards Uriahkles with full admiration, saying, "Hail, Caesar!" after which he takes his leave of them.

The physician, confident in their privacy, resumed his thoughts. "I, too, must leave. I am needed elsewhere, but remember my words, Uriahkles, for I once had a son; he was very much like you, and what the gods spared, man speared. I had one chance, one last precious chance to hold him tight again, but Rome was hungry, and did not allow either of us to visit each other, before it was too late. When I saw my son again, all that remained was his mangled body. I told my wife not to look upon him for fear of her fragile nature, but love overtook my counsel, and she saw what had happened to her last child. She was tired of mystery, and needed reality. She had her wish fulfilled, and to this day she does not remember my face, let alone her own name. Life, this they took from my son when they separated his soul from his body, but life they took from my beloved when they separated reason from her mind! I have given everything to something that has given nothing in return. I cannot allow it to happen ever again, not as long as I have the power to read and the will to think. I ask that you keep this secret, for I know, as you must now, how the world naturally misunderstands our struggles; it is unfortunate, but inevitable. Rest, Uriahkles, and may the gods, whose wills are mysteries, continue to execute their duties to you as well as to your family."

With these truths revealed, the healer, this sonless father, leaves the tent, dragging his bodyweight like soldiers carrying the wounded over their backs.

Pain had managed to build a device, and it reflected light from neighbouring sources which were near, and about the heart. Uriahkles refuses to relinquish unto his memory belief; how is it possible that the gods could give him such contrary natures, a history defined by pure extremes, infinite pain and definite comfort? So by this little ingenuity, fate managed to read the book of his longing, without resorting to the risk of actually having given him happiness. Uriahkles saw what had been done, and soon became apprehensive, but he is resolute. The small but curious contraption of fate is not to be successful in returning him to the business of barbarous bloodshed. The snaking semblance of doom in his father's face must have found likeness in the physician's, as so it did in his movements.

In his heart Uriahkles intuits a disposition diseased by war, so much so that he can't even remember a time when he actually believed in the oaths he took. Truth, he thinks, is gradually awakening in him, becoming cankerous so to such strength as to worry him greatly. The experience is registered, realised and thus redefines all previously held preconceived notions. It is similar, he intuits, to acquiring the freshness of some fine weather, having so secured its promise thus; he has finally come out of a foul shell. But the event did happen, but only in such a way that it appeared to have snatched knowledge of its sharp bitterness, which might have caused him to return to the protective shied of his shell. This occurred no differently than an indefinite self-imposed exile. So it never did happen. But it did. It was the end, which had only a beginning but never the promise of its hating antithesis. The soldiers are the elements; the war is that of nature. To be born is to become a soldier, what greater war can there exist? The weaponry is sickness, war and death; to occupy and be unable to underline the shadows of the heart is defeat. Illusion. Time and incuriosity: great enemies.

The words he had earlier heard have stapled a simple but sincere affection upon him. The wound is wounded by its memory, his aversion to the public blood-baths sown. The great ocean is before his eyes. There is but purpose in frail memory, for in that stale flame, wherein lies no warmth, nor any heat, burns the wood to ash, despair, and to the dust, which are forgotten deaths. Innocence is strangled by the blood-dripping hands of ignorance, which are hauntingly free. The ignorant are the true murderers.

He falls asleep, dreaming about liberty, freedom and war for none. It is not to last, however.

Uriahkles is awoken by a disturbance; a passer-by has dropped a variety of armours and armaments upon the muddy ground. The tent was familiar to habit, but not to nature. His eyes wander, with no clear intention or expectation except for food for causing disgust and paradox to argue in his stomach.

Restless nature is not the same as reckless character. This he thus contends.

The camp is repulsive, an institution of expanded illness ailments, a lie, lonely, lavish, lethal; a savage ontological orthography. He rises from bed, adorns his person with a robe of fine furs and ornamentations, and begins pacing. This activity, done anxiously, persists for quite some time until–at long last–he decides to raise his hand to lift some of the over-hanging curtains, which obstruct his vision of the camp.

He sees soldiers, young men such as himself, some even younger, collecting wood for the fire. Perusing the distance, but maintaining alertness for any approaching passer-by, he also sees sword fighting, practices common at this hour of the day. He hears horseback riding, arguments over the proper procedure of archery, sentinels by the way atop the enclosing fortifications; difficulties in strategising present itself to his intuition, the trenches have been dug recently, and mapmaking, he intuits, is also required. Uriahkles returns his watchful gaze to the original revelation that he had been a witness to.

He sees the fire warming their hands as the sword empties their minds of interconnectedness. He suspects himself of wanting to return to the intimate atmosphere of his compatriots, a desire which only the initiated, no matter how disillusioned, may understand. Isolate humanity, organise the affairs of State, collect the souls, build up the territorial integrity and stimulate obedience amongst the provinces. This, Uriahkles understands, is their duty, the purpose for which they became what they are now: soldiers. Conscience, they think, adulates their efforts; the people laud their valour, venerates them to the point of deification, so as to invite no distinction between the two, conscience and the conscious satisfaction they have taken and are taking in adulation. Uriahkles is affected. The affinity he feels with them is strong, inviting; and sombre contemplations cannot dissuade his affection from longing to return to them now. To end his self-imposed expulsion from public service, this affront to traditional values and standards, he ceases certain contemplations. Still, the desire to adorn his head with the steel helmet remains. The body's burning impulse to be touched by the uniform returns, for each stressed sense desires its counterpart. The eyes crave to capture the legions as they march to battle. The ears aspire to hear the anthem, the patriotic songs sung by compatriots. The instrument of scent feigns patience for the flagrant fragrance of combat. Touch is swallowed up by registering the sense of felicity, which is indeed garnered, by lifting the gladius; and thrusting her into the unsuspecting bosom of the attendant enemy. And indeed taste itself yearns for the flavour of foods and wine after the exertions of war, for the soldier's palate appears to multiply, and in no uncertain way, the delicious Italian dish sevenfold.

"My father, owing to his son, has now come to claim pride as bride to his reputation's midnight bed-chamber." Uriahkles overhears this from one of the seasoned soldiers in the distance nearby. He returns to his bed, and reclines, deciding to explore further the expanse of his unchecked want to return to his former life of service, duty and self.

The soldiers by the fire now begin to sing songs, commemorating Roman history, ingenuity, and the unconquerable of her true self, which is to rule over the world, and Romanise it.

Time is against him, and so the banquet, to be held in his honour, is soon to commence. What is he to do? Play the fool, and forget virtue in order to sustain life, which may enable him to pursue it further and teach this to others, spreading truth like wildfire in the wilderness of ignorance. What good is a martyr if he is unable to teach the living an example of how virtuous conduct preserves the quality for which he himself has lost? There is enough time allotted to death, but rarely enough for life. How is he to continue when soon he shall be called upon to speak handsomely of the City of the Seven Hills, to encourage the sons she has put in harm's way? He shall be called upon to glorify the Roman military machine, to heap numerous adulations upon it like so many dead bodies to the gravesite: piled, buried and forgotten. And certainly he shall have to speak generously of the gluttonous nature of the emperors. This he must not do, for it would be a violation, most hideous, of all that he now stands for. He cannot praise the devil in order to pray to God.

But he loves Rome, and here is where contradiction begins to take hold. Though imperfect, with as much faults to her register as night-fires in paradise, she is still the mightiest of all nations: past, present and future; a beacon of order to the world, a light with which we may hope to survive the perpetual night of nature, from within and without. Uriahkles continues to discourse in this strain. He recalls her gifts to her citizens. He begins by noting the creation of an effectual government. He then continues with the fashioning of Latin, a language of the arts and sciences. A sound currency system soon follows in his speech, which enables the Romans to have the greatest economy anywhere in the civilised world. In commerce, trade and industry the Empire is unmatched. Extended highway systems connecting us to the most far-flung regions in the empire: thus truth declares, "All roads lead to Rome!"; an efficient postal service, bridges, aqueducts, temples, courts, ministries, theatres, the beauty of her art and architecture; the emblem adorned with beautiful blessings of the gods created, manifested in the mighty empire is she. Uriahkles, however, does not forget what made these wonders possible, slave labour. Rome is an empire which is built on the backs of slaves, and thus her nature is in accordance to brutish philosophies and savage spiritualities. How shall he find peace in that which would fall to pieces, were it not for slavery, bloody conquest, ruthless ambition and the cold bureaucracy it came to create? Is this possible?

The answers to these questions escape him, and no matter how close he came to cracking their mystery, any such advancement is interrupted, when the good doctor requests permission for entering the tent. The mind is affected, but altered.

"May I enter, Uriahkles?" asks the physician.

His response is barely audible, "Come, please."

The healer continues, "I understand you are due shortly, so I shan't keep you long. My instructions are to see you ready, that is, to inspect your constitution and render an appropriate judgement regarding the degree to which you may participate in the evening's festivities. I expect all is well—" at which point Uriahkles interrupts him.

"No, it is not. The matter, if I may call it such, concerns my vocation. Justice is the beggar in my conscience. Shall I stay my hand, advance not pity or prayer, and abdicating the throne of mercy, turn my face away? Say now, and let he who have loved, and he who have laboured, know that the blood of nations be upon them; for I cannot find peace in war anymore."

"Good God, I cannot believe this; how is it possible?"

"I trust I have disturbed the past, and made the future in its image," says Uriahkles.

To which the doctor replies, "My son, shortly before his death, expressed one last wish to be done in dedication to his beliefs. It was delivered to me by word of mouth."

"And what was it?" asks Uriahkles.

The answer is swift. "To free a warrior who has freed himself from war," he pauses, shaken and solemn, resuming when he could. "Please understand what I have begun to acknowledge, do not think that the man, who stands before you now, is for want of redemption: far from it. It is rationality. Rationality is what I want—" At this point the physician, the imperturbable man of Asclepius, as many are for want of calling him, is unable to continue, so he stops in order to search the soldier's face.

Uriahkles, affected as he is, advances his question, "When you look at my face now, it is not mine which you see, is it, but your son's?"

"Yes," says the doctor, quietly.

"Then you will help me," says he.

"I cannot answer differently."

"Good, very good. I thank the gods for giving me such a gift. What truer healer among men there be now than he who stands here before me, remains kept from me, there's no such healer," says the son.

"And I thank them for doing no differently than what they have done to you," says the father.

"Tell me," asks he, "what is your name?"

"My name is Eurythikles."

Now Uriahkles, before advancing necessity presses for further acumen, "What has war taught you; I mean, simply, what has been revealed to you?"

The healer answers, saying, "War is the eternity of fools, but peace is the gift of genius. This, Uriahkles, is what I have been taught by my sufferings. I have to go."

Left to himself—all he must do now is wait for the hour of the festival. The hours, a pack of wandering wolves, have succumbed to sleep, their dreams being when darkness came that evening.

Walking out of one tent to go in search of another, Uriahkles welcomes the cool change of atmosphere. It is twilight, and the last glares off Apollo's diadem have begun to vanish over the darkening horizon. The encampment, he is led to consider, now rests not in an acerbic response to boredom, but in the moderate repose of prospect.

Nearing the tent, where the festivities are being held, he considers his stature. He knows that to invite doubt to his demeanour, let alone his visagial circus, would certainly permit for treacherous thoughts as regards his character, but especially to his loyalty to Rome.

Waiting by the entrance stands Eurythikles.

"Hello again, Uriahkles. I have made known my judgement as to your physic, which, as I have explained to the general, is tenuous but improving. He has rendered an official decision, and it is in your favour. However, since you pressed me to give you leave of absence awhile, so providing you with the necessary time in order to excuse yourself from the more enthused activities, and considering further your request to give the men public address, I too have informed the general as to your desire, and he was all but delighted to hear it. With the intent to perfect this fiction, I intoxicated his vanity with authority and admiration for you. I explained that were it up to me, I would not grant the request, but since I am in no such position to do so, I have brought the matter before the general, whom, as you may imagine, was seized by pride the extent to which I have not time to express. He commanded me to extend his warmest wishes to you

"Now, once you have entered the tent you shall be expected to advance yourself towards the general's table, and from hence, to deliver your speech. This done, I beseech you to rest yourself with food, innocent beverage, and light excursions, perhaps, into Greek mythology, after which I shall retrieve you for further inspections in preparation for a goodnight's rest."

• • • • • •

Entering the tent, Uriahkles is conscious of the sense stung by silence—is fast to feel how hundreds of eyes are pressing against him. The spectators are enamoured to be in the presence of a modest man, a disciple now of Hercules none other barely begun of his twenty-seventh year, so unlike that to which they became accustomed, with this particular emotion bearing no uncertain emphasis back in the Senate. Footsteps echoing in the memory, Uriahkles is reminded now of the gladiatorial games by reason of the spectatorship; for if the immortal spirit be the carcass from which they fuel their feast, they're feeding from off his flesh a vultured-proportion, impatient yet unlike the vulture which they share a still anguished likeness. Desire, envy, necessity, grudging admiration, bestial kindness, certain passion; these constitute the centre at which Uriahkles has found himself. Though taking prudence by the hand, he acknowledges his peers by gentle motions of the head, occasionally uttering some greeting, until he reaches the General's table, upon which he's promptly greeted.

"Welcome, Uriahkles. Honour has me now in one of his highest halls, by having you sit beside me."

"The honour is a joint-spoil, General Doulpsyche."

"Now, Uriahkles, it being the case that Apollo's son has jealously stolen you away from a good deal of the festivity, though by no means its entirety, have come at an occasion most suitable—as say I must—especially when now I am called upon to reconstruct, and in no uncertain manner, the object wherewith had concerned our symposium prior to your desired arrival."

"I trust you speak of war, General Doulpsyche," says Uriahkles.

"I do, indeed."

"Considering the rebuilding of your edifice, I shall posit a piece of contemplation, if I may do so."

"Most certainly, Uriahkles," answers he.

"Having discussed in some great detail the history of warfare, after securing confidence as regards the rise and fall of empires, you now wish to delve deeper within the warrior than in his art, perhaps by invoking the Muse, so as to tell us of some article from experiment which has informed you about the more subtle aspects of our dread occupation."

Finishing his reconstruction of their symposium, Uriahkles sees his neighbours shaking their heads in agreement, and poking their kin so as to indicate their pleasure in the young man's intelligence. Doulpsyche does no differently. Rising, then, to his feet, assuming a relaxed though yet somehow rigid posture, he commands the attention now of all who have gathered in the tent to hear him speak. He begins:

"I need to know nature before I could ensure its perseverance. What is the nature of the empire; how is war imperative in her design? The answer came to me when I began to understand the verses of my father, Maximus. He did not intend to consider civilisation, but the fire of Prometheus burned deep within him, and thus the affair was altered. My father answered my questions in a parable which has for its argument the Trojan Horse; that same old sinister device of Achaean conquest. He began his tractate with Odysseus, to whom Morpheus, acting on the commands of Jupiter, bequeathed reverie, this being the currency with which he was to bargain the imagination.

"The Greek from Ithaca found himself alone in his dream. The mighty armies Menelaus had commanded were nowhere to be found: departed, disappeared, devoured by Mnemosyne. The shore, he explained to himself, which had been sick once with the weight of a thousand ships, was untouched and bear of mortality. The sea into which the blood of soldiers had flowed freely was pure, infinitely pure. The waters were quiet, and quietness now reigned over the kingdom of lamentation. My father writes:

Where are the armaments of soldiery?
Is not the ground whereon I stand Death's plantation;
Is not the sea I see the hungry realm of Neptune,
The epitaph cracking frenzied incantation:
The self-substantial slaughter of nature?
Here do I but think of solemn frenzy.
Is this dear nature's bounteous silence?
Did the earth, poor mattress maiden, on sheets
Clean to innocence lost in what war devours
Expose hell to catch the children of chaos?
What ague, tribute, affection, passion may
Shrivel by time the sanction of such neglect?'
And he answered, saying,
I shall away to the abyss,
Doomed to hard nature's hand make plea,
For the mortal realms shall I see
Until Ulysses in loss hath Ulysses found!
Then vision came to pass:
Great Priam's City! thou shalt my gift partake,
Thus unto thee shall I impart heartache.
He makes prologue, but is soon the epilogue:
The sign, you shall see, is nature's folly.
Let not reason sleep,
Stay the hand of felicity awhile,
And bear thou witness to eternity!
My nature's of thine own, and shall inherent thee.
I shall build thee an awful sacrifice,
There hope old Abram hath with none left now to spare.
'Tis incisive, mark!
And thus shall I as thee fall deep asleep
And think the abhorrent against myself.

"The Gods themselves are not free from war, but nor is war free from them. We, the race of flesh and soul, are too not free from war, but it is free from us. In those terms, as thus encompassed by desire, my need is to secure Rome all the God's entitlements. I am, as you, the architects of history. For is not architecture an inescapable art, and the architect the most enduring, if not the greatest, of all poets of space? The conceiver of ubiquitous vision; inescapable is my art, it is the most persuasive of the human endeavours because the deed is done to facilitate the testaments of elegance, beauty, simplicity and necessity, which greatly objective, is crystallised in the dreams, desires and deeds of the visionary.

"I thought its adamantine qualities were godly, but now I have imposed upon myself a different account. I am advocating a petition concerning the matter, so that I may alleviate my mind from the altercation. This causes understanding in the mind, ameliorating the perception of my bedroom walls–appeasing, seasoning–allowing the visual feast to have more astuteness now than it had ever had before.

War is the glorious bureaucracy of belonging, and, being thus, it is the essential gladius with which to penetrate the obedient chaos towards the within.

"We are soldiers, men for whom order is inevitable. Negotiation is dissuasive to the soul, belittling my valour! It was compatible, possibly persuadable, to obedient chaos. The enemy engineers adjustment, thus allowing interpretation: this leads to tempting illusions. The politics of Rome are not of our concern. The Senate is the Emperor's mistress. The matter is clothed in uncertainty, but impressed upon the legislative body, this is not to last—for soon the laws are laid down, rough hue them Your Majesty, and the policies are buttressed thus. The law is to be disseminated by a violent hand. There is no god who has not imposed upon his people the threat of accordant destructions. Divine justice, if such a thing there be, is rage most pure, universal, violent, and wholly natural. I find it ironic how the old moral philosophers described anger as a brief madness, casting the passion unkind terms in their numerous, often differing teachings on the matter. Anger binds god to himself, and so allows the good to be at home with itself. The passions of the soul, which are analogous to political taxes, are for want of collection. They are collected by anger. The affairs of reason and nature impose upon us the need for organisation. In the process and product of anger, it sets them upon the true path of an organised constitution. The industry of civilisation is then foundational. Anger, rage, fury, wrath; these are features, specifically the features of the face of Justice herself, and so the violent hand of its administration is savage, swift and simple.

"War's a meditation on justice!

"We stand in the shadows of uncertainty, but are called upon to drag out our enemies into the light, and there we have fought them.

"I saw some light twinkling atop the Forum once, its roofed corner, most of the ceiling was gone, swallowed up by the light. I thought how like soldiery this is! We illumine, and how do we achieve illumination? Simple. We present possibility to power, which causes Caesar to cross the Rubicon, which by another name is called history.

"Sons of Rome! My soldiers! Do not forget that we are the forgers of the Great City, and are as such destined to either define peace by war or war by peace. This is our lasting tribute to the City of the Seven Hills. We must never forget this.

"Now it is my distinct honour and duty to introduce you to Uriahkles, son of Neptonius, emblem of the Fasces!"

Rising to his feet, assuming a natural but imposing presence, Uriahkles begins his address, saying:

"There is a time when peace comes to pass, to establish dominion over our wars. Necessity is intolerable, but so is slavery. To be masters of nature is our truth, the purpose for which we have been chosen. In order to form a more perfect empire, this being the celebrated dream of the Caesars, we are called upon to bear arms against nature and nature's progeny. We divine order from chaos, potency from portents, divide realms into relics; conquer kingdoms, thrash at their flesh till from their kings we have made slaves of them; there is no fortress or citadel, army or navy, barrack, tactic, battalion, garrison or sovereignty over which we have not been triumphant. History, at least so say the historians in Rome, has been Romanised; it is the Emperor's most treasured province. We as Romans abhor failure, but are unconfident about our victories. Adversities present themselves as simplicities only; there is no want for want of argument. Indeed, merely by its semblance, they are troubles with a foundation in the expected, the accepted and the unexceptional, none to which we need bequeath Promethean fire. So in seeing these things, one may draw them out as inevitable, a duty for which we must risk freely.

"The virtue of valour is thus determined. It is interfaced indelibly with inevitability, an instance thereof, which arises, ascends, awakens but which also deepens, solidifies, makes profound the perceptions for which lives lived in the amusing opera of the ordinary trash out respect, the good that the good-at-heart inherently assume in its agency. There are times when these things do come about, but there are other times when it does not, and should not.

"The movement with which we deny stillness longevity is ironic, for she shall then provide us abundantly with what we gave scarcely. We monument this fact in our art and architecture, but particularly in the great palaces of the Caesars. The history of Rome is an instant, the breaking of a few strings, lost love it is as has, so far, been explained the moment at which the gladius is struck into the bosom, severs limb, mangles cartilage and bone, as so to produce the last kiss, now firmly impressed upon the lips: a naked body eternally. The mere musical monotony of a minute opens up a certain change, great in its extreme, profound in its purpose to the bloodied conscience, which is gradually awakened in the combatant. The time necessitated for its appearance is indefinite, and therefore uncertain.

"Was not Troy orphaned to Italy, and the she-wolf mother of the brothers, one of whom later became the founder of Rome?"

Uriahkles pauses briefly, then resumes:

"The world has orphaned itself to oblivion, and Rome, the she-wolf of civilisations, has become matriarch of the muses; patriarch of the souls of men!"

The applause deluges the senses, and absorbing their courtesy, having secured their favour by reason of history, he now takes his leave of them.

Capturing some fresh air, and tossing his gaze around, Uriahkles is pleased to see the doctor upon his exodus from the tent. The physician is quick to speech.

"Word has reached me from Rome. His Majesty, rendering his decision in accordance to your father's request, in addition to His ambition, has promoted you to the office of procurator over the province, which, as you must know, is Judea. I trust that the subtlety has not escaped you."

Uriahkles is certain, remarking further:

"Judea is doomed. The insurgent, insubordinate province is now insufferable. It is widely held that conquest is unavoidable, and so being procurator of Judea ensures its occupier the vocation of hunting, executing and other like epicurean pursuits. The Emperor is sure to provide a handsome battalion in defence of my person during my sojourn in Judea. My time shall be spent, if time there be, in chasing the wind or arguing about the true shape of Proteus. This ensures my vigour, which, as you surely must have expressed it in your correspondence with the Emperor, requires heavy insurance; especially when considering the extent to which I was injured during battle, wherein I not only proved my valour, but indeed demonstrated my loyalty and duty to His Majesty. Continuing the discourse in this strain, considering the advantage of having me returned to Rome, not in dust and ash but in conscious flesh, your impartial testimony, shall we say, and taking into account the reputation my father enjoys as a profound expert in the laws, some of which, mark, were written by the man atop the throne, the Emperor has made me procurator over a forsaken people. Reason is naked, and the outcome inevitable."

"Is this to say that you shall accept?"

"Do I have a choice?"

"Then it's settled. Your father and mother shall be delighted. I shall send word back to Rome at once."

Uriahkles pauses, breathing in such a way as to appear not breathing at all. He resumes:

"I must now return to my quarters, repose, and prepare for the journey whose embarkment now appears certain. Yes, then Judea it is.

"Good night, doctor."

"Good night, procurator."

• • • • • •

"Is all in order, Centurion?"

"Yes, Sire."

"Then Peace let me be, and I shall see you anon."

"Hail, Caesar!"

"Is this the land which clashed against a thousand gods, and wept God to silence for all eternity?" asks Uriahkles; "Guard, send for one of my consultants."

"Yes, Sire."

Uriahkles hears himself asking the same question, again and again: "I wish to better my knowledge of Judea but how?"

"Good evening, my lord," greets the consultant, interjecting a stormy stream of reflection. Continuing to communicate his carnivorous curiosity, however, Uriahkles resumes his strain of thought.

"I have heard that by your veranda, upon nightfall, there congregates a certain group of Jews whom by their title are called Pharisees. Their leader, an eccentric so-called by the Hebrews, particularly by the sons of Aaron, has made it his custom to recount stories of the governorship of Judea under Herod the Great. His faction of Judaism is traditional by temperament, but iconoclastic as a result of the teachings taught during their congregations.

"What is the name of their instructor?"

"His name, my lord, has not been revealed, and all attempts to divine it have, so far, proven disastrous. The Cohanim, however, have begun to call him Sharhanim Ben Shemot."

"In Hebrew, unless I am mistaken, but I am not, his name means Sharhanim, Son of the Names."

"Yes, Sire."

"When did Sharhanim and his circle begin their practice of congregating by the overhang?"

"My dread lord, since word first spread of your arrival to Judea."

"I trust that with respect to Sharhanim, I shall be within an audible range."

"It is assured, Sire."

"Then bid the municipal powers to make haste. I wish the veranda and all precincts immediate to its border unburdened of whatsoever presence but my own."

"Then it shall be as you say, my liege."

"Now go, and please be orderly in your appointment; for I do not seek to have distraction invited to my interrogation of this truant sect of Jews."

"Yes, Sire."

Uriahkles is restless, and does not tear himself apart from his desire.

"How I grow in desire to know of these people! What, am I enslaved by my desire to have dominion over certain mysteries, to know history's designs; when has the race of men ever been freed from such bondage?"

Removing himself to the veranda, Uriahkles is accompanied only by a few oil lamps and thrice as many shadows. He paces the time away.

Then he sees them; they have made a circle around the person of Sharhanim. Their leader addresses them, saying:

"Evil had once ruled this land with a mighty hand and an outstretched arm. Herod was its manifestation. His eyes were not journeying liberally; he was deeply concentrated, intoxicated-deep with desire and necessity, between which he drew no immediate distinction.

"His mistrust was profounder than any sea lying on the earth, deeper in dimension and darker in its intention. His obsession for entitlement was indefatigable, but the means by which he pursued political power were sudden, savage, and regimented.

"He was the progeny of converts, forced converts that is. There's little prefix in my expression as to how troubled I am to myself when I contemplate nature's disturbing industry.

"This is what I understand because the unwritten chronicles of this period in our history have impressed my heart thus.

“Fear is easily concealed, but terror abducts the eyes when such rootless orbs have looked upon it. Herod’s subjects could not have lost this chain of thought or the tide thereof, for as they prayed to God, the material self of malevolence sat upon the throne of Jerusalem, great King David’s city. For that reason it was imperative to combat destructive history with a devouring faith, at least so thought the Jews of the time.

“I am speaking of the worse, when I shall speak of what came to pass in the land, which God gave us. So much of what could have happened did happen, but all failed when it was happening, and thus what has happened, happened, but it could have happened in any other way. The tragic history was preventable; that is why it is tragic.

“Hold fast to your affection, fortify felicity; be secured in your faith, in order that I may recount the hideous hiddenness of God’s creation.

“It began in the capital. There were two doctors whom the whole nation esteemed for their reputation as profound experts in the laws of their fathers. These men, of whom the name of the one was Judas, son of Sepphoraeus; and the name of the other Matthias, son of Margalus; having heard word of the king’s decline, had chosen to emphasise a particular abomination which the king had committed against the laws by exercising their speech to enlighten the public. Their pronouncements attracted, particularly, men in their prime; and as the quality of their speeches became grander; so did the quantity of their listeners become greater. With word of the king’s failing constitution firmly impressed upon their minds, their lectures began to throw out hints that the time was ripe for avenging God’s honour. As you know, it is unlawful to place in the temple graven images, whether these are, as for example, busts or tapestries; because representations of whatsoever living creature is seen as strictly sacrilegious. Herod was not detracted, however, and advanced his architects to erect over the great gate a golden eagle. The abomination long since done, the king not quite undone, it was this impious symbol that they exhorted their disciples to remove from reality forever. The doctors made sure practice in nullifying the fear of death in their listeners, claiming that to die in defence of the law of one's country would ensure their souls the attainment of immortality, lasting honour to their progeny, and a deathless consciousness of felicity. Death with meaning is not death, but a privilege of rarity for which we must struggle; for it is only the ignorant, the ignoble and the men of great spiritual illness, dead in themselves, who clung in their folly to life, and preferred death on a sick-bed to that of a hero. The award of martyrdom is eternity.

"Such words poured forth from their mouths into the hearts of their listeners. Continuing to discourse in this strain, accident joined ruin in the form of a rumour, which had begun to spread. It was rumoured that the king was dying; the angel who had taken the firstborn away from Egypt, was about to take Herod out of the Great City. The rumour caused the men to enact the words of their teachers, and so at midday, when many people were perambulating the temple, they began their impassioned enterprise. Atop the roof, they let themselves down on stout cords, and finding themselves before their prey, they began chopping off the golden eagle, Rome's presence, with hatchets. The act was seen at once and the captain, time swift in its march to have the matter reported to him, hastened to the scene with ire, never you mind an eye-flooding force. Many were arrested, and many more had escaped.

"The captured were brought before the king in shackles. Herod asked three questions. The first was indulgent. "Did they dare to cut down the golden eagle?" They admitted it. Second, he asked for the identity of the chief instigator(s) who had given the order. The answer they provided him was thus: “The law of our fathers.” Now during the entire period of the interrogation, Herod was fully aware of the felicity in the faces of the captured. Indeed, their very tones of voice, mannerisms, and general demeanour were all indicative of a joyous disposition. This amused the king so much so that he ended his interrogation with this question, “Why so exultant, when we shall shortly pronounce you dead?” To which they replied, “Because after a brief interruption, which you call death, we shall enjoy such great felicity that compared to it, all earthly kings appear but as wanton beggars.”

“Incensed with abysmal anger, the king hastened them to their deaths.

“Death is approaching Herod, one great tyrant to another. The builder of the Temple is said to have meditated thus:

“Idolatrous fools all! What the pagans made out of earth, air, fire and water, they shall transmute out of scroll, tablet, papyrus, and the like matter, and into such insubstantial stuff as papyri, tablets and scrolls, until from prayer as a means to God, it is itself god; godless, gratuitous, gluttonous gruesome idolatry, a pale purpose, forsooth!

“The Jews in purpose have Abram’s god slain! For is it not cruel, calculated and unnatural that we are to consider, that the felicity of this life, the observance of God’s commandments, given by God to Moses at Sinai, consists not in the very purpose for which the prayer had begun! it is as if the Jew had transmuted the Golden Idol into the pure gold of a Torah scroll! They worship not god, but the book in which they claim to have found God! the very item of revelation in which we find instructions for worship became worshipped, the warnings against idols are idolised themselves, for where you pray is prayer, your people are not my people, be they blood-people, your God is this god, Torah, yes! Is it any wonder then that it took a Herod to teach them a lesson, noble in intention and valuable in its instruction: to organise her affairs, to collect the taxes for Rome, build up her economy, and stimulate her trade. I returned the Temple, and made the religion exist not in the mind alone, but a living being in the land, a life-blood for the soul of Man? I saw what they did not, not because they could not, but would not, and thus God, for just such a want, should have made me king, did make me king, the sovereign over all the land which flows with milk and honey. My name is the name of God's will! But be warned, Israel, for while stands Herod, the House of David shall stand; but when falls Herod, the House of David shall fall; and when great David's House falls—the Temple. This is your exile."

••••••

Rome. A chamber in the palace, the Emperor is in speech with an officer, whom is charged now with the future carnage of Jerusalem.

"With which uniform, my liege, shall Mars delight in himself?"

"Time is a luxury which we may afford," says Caesar, "I intend to indulge myself accordingly. Making an allowance for mercy, we shall allow the Jews in Jerusalem to destroy themselves for that is how Mars most delights himself in war: when we merely aid the enemy in civil suicide."

"Shall you appoint His Highness to lead the war against the Jews?"

"Yes, of course. Our son, however, is still for want of a few yet more lessons. We shall, therefore, appoint for him an assistant who, familiar with the reigns of power, is quite experienced in assisting generals of lesser talent in such a sober campaign."

"And who shall His Grace favour?"

"Tiberius Julius Alexander, who had governed the province in question for two years; he knows how to fight a war."

"What quality, then, has His Highness?"

"We can trust him; especially when the mob persuades him of that."

"Then be it so. Hail, Caesar!"

• • • • • •

Imprisoned within himself, this child of chaos, Uriahkles, is oblivious to the men who have now attained political power. His counsel is deprived of audience with the men who are purely defined by their aim to end Roman occupation, thus returning autonomy for their beloved Zion.

The procurator of Judea has abandoned Caesar, and prayed to the Hebrew God, but now it is too late. Forced to lie down, as if asleep, unconscious of either himself or the universe, the grievous concussion whereby the procurator came to this state has torn him apart from the struggle.

The impolitic insurgents are founded solely on blind orthodoxy. Eleaser, son of Simon, has his zealots; and John of Gischala, a private army. They strive together for political freedom, minting silver coins with the legend "Freedom of Zion." But soon a new leader has come to power, Simon bar Giora, who stands at the head of a messianic ambition; his metallic men have "Redemption of Zion" for their call to arms. Copper coins bearing this legend are soon circulating.

Time is taken from him, and thus begins the interminable wait for dear wake. Uriahkles lies asleep; his dream-content draws no distinction between life and art.

. . . suddenness . . . wakefulness . . . his eyes being opened now he begins to register movement and his environment; he's fettered . . . being transported by a sluggish wagon, and all around him are bronze bars, not here—

Still, he seeks answers from a fellow prisoner.

"How did Rome appear before the Hebrews?" asks Uriahkles, clearly aware of what has happened, war and defeat for the Jewish nation. His fellow replies:

"I am sickened by the numbers, but while we struggled to overwhelm their operations, there were specific legions with which I took much offence. Of these I hark back to XII Fulminata and XV Apollinaris. They shared a large camp to the northeast of the old city, on Mount Scopus. The former was a new addition from Syria. The V Macedonica was camped at a short distance. X Fretensis occupied the Mount of Olives; mind you, fate had especially fuelled their incentive to fight. I trust you know why, my dear procurator."

He answers, saying, "The Zealots had defeated them before, leaving them shamed-face to their alien gods. Revenge, however, became their god and they were eager to pay homage to their new deity by smashing all the reminders of their gross humiliation."

"In this, Uriahkles, you are most approved."

The procurator remarks further, "I trust that some petty kingdoms, these vultures of history, had extended their hand in allegiance to Rome in order to cooperate in the destruction of Jerusalem."

"They came in the form of Commagene and Emesa, two vulture kingdoms on the Upper Euphrates."

Uriahkles, though not surprised at all with which company Rome chose to accompany itself during the struggle, remains nonetheless touched, his thoughts expressed as much, "The Arabian sheik has deep hatred in his heart for your people. It very much worries me how the Arab tyrants are quick to join the Romans with their warriors. They are harlots of death, who have no shame in proselytising themselves to their black impulses, which are fuel for the frenzied feasts of demons."

Agreeing with his assessment, the prisoner adds, "Their banquets do not go unattended, for there came from Italy many criminals. They were veterans from the defeated armies of Galba and Otho. Their aim was simple: murder the innocent along with the combatants, devour no less greedily than fire, and violate the honesty of the Holy Land with their idolatry. Against such forces, the besieged in Jerusalem stood little if no change at all.

"The General was Titus, but the mind of the war was in the person of his assistant, Tiberius Julius Alexander. He was, like you, a former governor of Judea. And so it was.

"Passover came, bringing with it Titus." He pauses, interrupted by violent chuckles; subdued, he then departs from hope to continue his story, "Striking too short at dread, whom I grasp an appalling irony no other, Titus began the siege during Passover." A soft wind caresses his cheek now, pausing briefly he now resumes again; "Jerusalem, my brother, Jerusalem was being violated during a time when the Hebrew God himself had sent death, sleep's black simulacra, to lay siege upon Pharaoh's hardened heart."

"Tell me about the city. How did chaos calculate her borders?"

"Simon was charged with the defence of the Old Town. As you know, she lays situated atop a steep plateau in the south. The walls ornamenting her integrity faced the Valley of Hinnom in the west and south; they were old but rebellious to conquest. The violent persuasions of the catapult could not move her, at least not until the very end."

"How many men did Simon command?"

"He commanded ten-thousand Hebrew warriors and five-thousand Idumeans."

"Distrust, discourtesy, and discontinuity defined these men, didn't it?" he observes, more than asking.

"It is the great tragedy wrought by this war that we could not trust ourselves. Division of the land was pale in comparison to the division of the soul. From the east of the Temple complex, where stood two-thousand four-hundred of Eleaser's Zealots, to the west of that region, occupied by six-thousand men of John's militia, there were just as many doubts, fears and distrust as there were units of distance between their lines of defence. It is telling how with respect to the zealots, I mean the inner bulwark, there was near them the Kidron ravine, the object in whose presence you prevented any enemy attack. Imposing fortifications in the form of protective walls, Uriahkles, are shadows to those erected in the hearts and minds of a people. For they assume the form of chaos, which makes orphans of us all. The city is isolated from the world by reason of the barricade, but its citizens are insulated within themselves, starved and are forced to wander around their own souls, until, from exhaustion, they perish by reason of the self-stockade. This is actually an ingenious but grotesque form of self-inflicting death, a slap to the face of God. We were men of Bibles written in blood, and the road to hell was paved with our souls. Did you know where this road began to appear in the land, Uriahkles?"

"Grave scholar of truth, memory tells me that the part of the Temple complex of which you speak was a construction called Antonia, a castle of some great but proud disposition."

"Yes, to this lofty castle which we built within us we called ourselves kings. God did not abandon us, however. He did not need to, you see, because we were about to abandon ourselves.

"Passover came, striking too much the calendar with potent attentions that Eleaser did allow the inhabitants to honour their duties, and thus the Temple received their obligations. Just as Jerusalem sank deeper, so too did John cause to sink deeply the much-needed festivity of the hour: swords brandishing swordsmen. Threatening violence against an inferior viciousness, Eleaser and his zealots had then been forced into surrendering their authority, thus beginning a distrustful consciousness of disposition. Flushed with the spoils of victory, John called for a pre-emptive strike.

"He had reason to fear so as to sharpen this aspect into fervours for pre-emption. The Romans had now busied themselves in building new camps, these being west of the city: one for the legions XII Fulminata and XV Apollinaris and one for legion V Macedonica.

"An attack of this nature was imperative, but John feared Simon as much as Simon feared him. Had John given word for the attack, he, as did the majority of his men, did nestle deep within themselves deeper dread about Simon locking the gates behind their backs. Protesting perpetually, but falling on ears deaf to any future plea for re-entry; this was their fear.

"Time did soon teach them the folly of their dispositions, and so it was that the Romans built their camps, fresh threats to us, building a great many redoubts, and this almost–so I dare say–without any trouble, whatsoever. Thus impatient for attack, though sooner could it have come, much sooner! What, now, but this, the Latin legions for want of wooing the Queen of the Nations by taking the soldier's vows in their commitment for her destruction.

"The catapults, a dread emblem of the *Pax Romana*, had soon begun to violate the city, diseasing our defences with incurable wounds, nastier scars, and a few more lustful visions of an upcoming apocalypse. The hours and the minutes kept watch as heavy missiles, stones taken from sacred sites–so we are told–did catapult our kin further into desperation, dereliction and those grand heights in the demonic feats of the zealous-frenzied, with which much of the rest of the world is decorated, disturbed, then destroyed. Using this blood-cloud of artillery fire, the Romans began bashing the northern wall with their battering rams.

"This Roman attack did what ought to have been done by their merely being there, namely the unification of our people, all of whom were now securing sorties, busying themselves with valiant deeds of duty, not vicious derelictions thereof. This too was tardiness of our nature, and thus did folly dethrone our attempts in erasing their siege towers. This having passed, these monstrous agues bequeathed my men appalling apprehensions. Taller than walls, they enabled legionaries to throw missiles on its defenders; so precise was their plan that when we sought shelter from the missile, the battering rams began their work of indiscriminate slaughter. When fifteen days had passed, the wall succumbed to its violence, and collapsed, permitting Titus to mould his passion into great Hebrew blood shedding. We, then, withdrew from Bezetha to our second wall. Titus spoke accordingly, his orders being an all-out attack on this wall, where our defenders had yet remained unorganised.

"For four days and nights did John and Simon hold danger in their palms, four days of vast wild dark and four nights of immeasurable hope, but on the fifth day, when stillness became cold as death and silence disturbing as annihilation, the wall bowed to Titus, having ceded to the violence of the battering rams. We did not cease to believe in the faith of our fathers, and therefore continued to fight the enemy; New Town especially saw our defenders inflict losses most sad upon the Roman hordes. The certain sense of possibility spiralled about Jerusalem air, like solicitude around a lonely traveller looking across the wild desert expanse. The great deed was done, and we forced the Romans to retire through the breach to Bezetha. Take this from this, and with four days gone, so too was our victory. The enemy drove us away from the second wall, which was immediately put to destruction.

"Titus' army, wishing to smack the face of hope, ravished silence by holding a vociferous parade, violent in its dimensions, which lasts four days. Further insult comes by way of a son of Aaron, whom by another name is called Flavius Josephus. Titus persuades Aaron's son to petition their cause to the men atop the walls, acknowledging himself in like manner to Jeremiah, disturbing the dread quietness with calls for submission to God's newly chosen people. The leaders are not impressed by his speech, nor are they moved by his silence. The matter ends in defeat for Titus and his adviser.

"Dawn brings with it the fifth day, on which Rome rekindles the struggle for recapturing Peace's Citadel. The Latin engineers are quick in busying themselves with the construction of five large siege dams, all of which are aimed at Antonia. This fortress is sad in its purpose, especially since its existence secures large stores and two great cisterns.

"This too comes to failure. Our sappers did with salient skill undermine the dams, also managing in this valiant process to raise a fire on a second one. Time teaches the Romans the sadness of this failure when Simon's soldiers are triumphant in their task to raze the last three dams down as it is done but two days later. We were committed, Uriahkles, to fight for every inch of our city, not to abandon the promise for which we had been chosen. But tragedy was soon to strike triumph, and the blow was hard to our hearts, which had already been hardened. The secure flame of our supplies was cultivating fragility, instituting ominous signs for us but beginning hopeful indications to Titus and his men that we were on the brink of a long, bitter and violent stage of intolerable starvation. This was confirmed when some of our people had been driven out of the city by starvation, their hope being to find food in the valleys before the walls. Their fates were grotesque and ungodly for decent men of god-fearing disposition. The vast majority of them had been caught, and crucified. Reports were rampant that some five hundred every day met this hard fate. Atop the walls of Jerusalem, we saw what had already been done to them, our people! The soldiers–so I saw–had amused themselves by these crucifixions, their pleasure was greater erected when they began to nail their victims in different postures, making malicious motions of the bodies, permitting vultures to pick out their eyes, and maggots to make their Satanic nursery in their flesh. Nature, too, was to suffer.

"All majestic vegetation, especially the trees crowning the soil, within a certain radius of some great expanse, were stripped, torn down, and split in order to make further inventions, these being tools to be later used in our forced funerals. The Romans took what God had given us in order to make the weapons of their military operations, violating God's own hand against itself.

"Titus had now reorganised his machine, thus demolishing the camps of the legions V Macedonica, XII Fulminata and XV Apollinaris, billeting these troops on Bezetha.

"The Romans, owing oblivion yet one last offence, having so reformed necessity into wanton acts of carnality, had begun to bash the brain sombre bells of some great melancholy. Starvation and depravity were their instruments of war, and so laid dead whatsoever rule of engagement. We were, my dread compatriot, being starved into surrender. The third dawn done, the capital laid behind an eight-kilometre long palisade."

The prisoner struggled for some time, pausing as began he now persisting at once, begging time–so Uriahkles would have contended–in order to give voice to what he saw. When his story was finished, the wagons continuing their dusty journeys across the wilderness, Uriahkles understood how meaningless it had all been, the insurgency raised up against Rome.

He is abandoned to his imagination, each thought a deserted island from which there's no expectation of escaping. Jerusalem during the siege, how . . . death daily ate his disastrous Hebrew dish, a great feast for frenzied appetite, be it most certain! The rate at which the besieged were dying was increasing, and increasing greatly. Uriahkles imagines how the Kidron valley and the Valley of Hinnom, great areas, must have been soon forced to betray beauty by receiving deep into their outward wombs corpses of an appalling variety.

The prisoner also revealed to him of how verily at the first did defectors come to be. There's a story, in particular, which now occupies his troubled mind. One such child of despair came to Titus, telling proud Caesar's son that the Hebrew dead numbered no less—" he interrupts himself to scratch the figure down against the wood with sand, the modern Arabic equivalent of which is 115,880. "Desperation befell Jerusalem, my dread defector," so said the nameless prisoner, confiding in him once again. Day was all of a sudden turned into inmost blindness, and night the like became soon the abyss from which arose clearest revelation. There was no scarcity in black invention, no, nor unoriginality of horror which befell the desperate inhabitants of God's earthly capital. Like as the Jews made towards Abram's promise, when Moses in cool ecstasy had Pharaoh's word revealed, so too did people seek to leave Jerusalem. This is what the Roman saw.

These souls, alas, did not know what awaited them. For had they, by God's beneficence, secured success in passing their own lines, and had not been seen by Caesar's dread slaughtermen, patrols of effortful barbarism, they would reach, he recalled, the palisade. Here did they surrender, forfeiting all allegiance to the men whom they had pledged it. "God, so said the sons of Aaron, had abandoned us, and adopted Caesar's children; what prayer better to have prayed than us joining our successors?" was the questioned asked by the voices of the abandonment.

With their loyalties now secured, the prisoners were at last entitled to hope, that is, given some bread.

Uriahkles hears these prisoners in imagination the while, how they hadn't the means by which they could've drawn distinction between persuasion and starvation: and so hunger, the faculty by which we secure life and detain its counterpart, became in their hands the fate into which they'd been thrown, almost as if to see hungry death swallow them up whole.

He knew what they hadn't, remembering his experience in the armed services. A great many of them, these Jewish prisoners, having no prior knowledge of what awaited them, began to eat so much, that they soon contracted pains of the stomach. Further abandoned by either relief or comfort, they retired or were given over to certain peregrinations, about which lurked greater portents. And suddenly being overtaken by still greater spasms, their stomachs burst and then death came to them. Edacious injustice, however, did not stop there.

When this dismal spectacle befell reality, their oedematous bodies suffered further violation when their Syrian and Arabian warders slapped, slashed, and stashed what little integrity remained with the corpses. Their savage surgeries were the result of certain superstitions which informed them of how these people had swallowed precious metals, as for example coins, before commencing their god-crying crossing. Uriahkles contemplates how there is injustice in thinking their deaths deserved for defecting to Caesar's expectant camp. Do not forget that many great men of Torah defected from Jerusalem and into the hands of Rome, one of which prophesied to Titus his succession to the coveted throne, and another prostrating himself before Rome in order to tell his story, and befriend his Latin allegiances, all of which were now newfound.

Titus didn't punish these violators, thus violating international conventions. And Uriahkles was well aware as to why he had done this. Titus must've soon discovered that there were too many. The nameless prisoner had told him how he was told by one of his men that one of the defectors was an esteemed educator of the Laws, who lying about the condition of his constitution, deceiving the guards, and bargaining with the enemy by reason of magic arts, had saved his life: for this he shall cause the memory to be rekindled. What memories are these, Uriahkles does not know, and if he did, he would bury their secret deep within him. Never to be taken out.

The windless air reminds Uriahkles of how he had once build forts when there were no breezes. How strange, this did he think, that it might have been windless, when the new siege dams were built. The prisoner had told there was no wood left, and so it took the enemy engineers a fortnight and some seven days to complete their construction. The object of the siege dams was Antonia.

The blood is enthused before battle, and Uriahkles can almost taste their excitement when the warriors, fed and hungry, defeated their Jewish enemy, weak and hungry. The nightmare of the nightly violence of the battering rams was inescapable, and on one night, the Romans flirted with a taste of triumph.

The Jewish engineers had seen this coming, and the prisoner said they had been prepared. A wall of the Antonia yielded to the violence of the battering rams, but much, one would hope, to the bitter surprise of the legionaries, being greeted as they were by a new wall, which had been built behind the breach. The Romans, however, true to their murderous love, would discover other means of penetrating the beautified fortress.

And so it came to pass that during a dark August night, when sleep had befell many of the men, twenty-four Roman soldiers did what the dark alone enabled them to do. Uriahkles hears them climbing the walls of the castle; they killed the guard and declared their intentions by reason of the trumpet. The suddenness of the attack echoed a Trojan-Horse position of consciousness, and so it was that embarrassment led way to puzzlement. The number of enemies was overestimated, because the garrison of the Antonia had yielded to the violence of the suddenness of the attack. Fear forced the hand of history, and the puzzled populace began flooding the Temple in overwhelming numbers. The prisoner had said that from his post, he saw what he thought were ants fleeing from the anthill, not soldiers bravely engaged in sad military operations.

Uriahkles begrudgingly admits his admiration for how the enemy used our own devices against us. The mine that John's sappers had made for several of the causes was now the royal road through which the enemy entered inevitability. Deep in the dark morning, the fortress was penetrated. In mere hours they who had entered through the hateful hole had driven John's men away. By this time the Romans had taken a great many prisoners, to which they attached much utility. The hard hand of fate forced the priests in the Temple to interrupt the daily sacrifices, greatly demoralizing the men, the last defenders of Jerusalem. As far as Uriahkles was concerned, this was the beginning of the end. The proud fortress was razed to the ground, and the Antonia became mere memory.

The birds were silent, the road that led to hope demolished, irrational love lost in a bewildering wilderness. Not a stone was left unturned because the Romans used them to build a new dam. The direction toward which it faced was the Temple terrace. The eventual violence was formidable, but failed to cause the walls to yield to their impatient agenda—Uriahkles pauses, but disgust disguised as disgrace dishonours this demeanour, so he resumes by stepping over ruins, continuing to imagine. By the last days of the struggle, the Temple itself was burning. The blood of eight thousand Zealots was spilled, at the Court of the Gentiles the prisoner said he saw six thousand women and children taken as prisoners, while the legionaries, despite the short threat of fire, sacrificed to their alien gods in the Holy of Holies.

What happened to John of Gischala and Simon son of Giora? He remembers asking, to which the prisoner replied:

"They rekindled negotiations with Titus, and began burning for a different fate. They petitioned Titus for permission to leave the city, further requesting the release of their troops. Faith informed their actions, especially when I recall their quoting Zechariah who had foretold a time in which we would see our city sacked, our women raped, liberty banished, and freedom slain. In their hour of dark they sought light in the guise of divine intervention, believing that by abandoning their metropolis of ghost and ash, they would pave the road for Abraham's God."

"So, Titus spurned their prophetic desires and left them to their fates."

Yes, Uriahkles said to Uriahkles, after which the Romans advanced their campaign of doomsday by destroying the quarter immediately south of Herod's Temple, reducing the great archives to inconspicuous dust, so much more ashy forgetfulness. The building where the Sanhedrin convened was now no more real or imaginary—so he should have it to semblance—than the forgetful Pharaoh of Egypt, under whom our ancestors laboured and were liberated by reason of the exodus.

This done, they proceeded to the Old Town, where they continued their murderously visionary orgy. There were a few defenders still hiding themselves in the sewer system, like so many other rats fleeing from the frenzy, but they too surrendered, amongst whom John was the first. Simon followed, haunting the grounds on which the Temple had stood. Sporting his sombre garb, a priestly tunic accompanied by his royal purple mantle, he surrendered on the birthday of his daughter Julia; thus Titus became conqueror of what was left of Jerusalem.

Finishing what may never be finished, the procurator, the survivor of the Jewish struggle did not speak again, but wrapt his voice in continual prayers, none of which would be extinguished until death had parted them. The ride to Rome continued, and Uriahkles, exhausted by grief, surrendered his senses to a sleep sombre in its awake, dreaming of a yet more bewildering savagery.

A lion in the desert distance roars, this reawakening Uriahkles. Having regained consciousness, to wit it appears as if he is sleep, and as sleep wrapt his senses, this ambiguous state, like some grand receptacle, was the bottomless jug into which poured all the profound misery and monotony of Rome. Roman sentinels bound him to the standards due to some anonymous though yet almost heinously haughty criminal, and night maintains to reign over the ethereal abyss. He stands now before an imperious spokesman, his face expressionless, the speech thrust with arrogant emotion.

"Good morning, Procurator," says he, the tone dry like desert, low, and limp.

Uriahkles replies no differently, "Why is the Senator not with his mistress, such ungodly hour as it is, surely you were stirred by Caesar none other, indulging virtue as you do time. Awaking thus is the sign of a discerning serpent in Rome; I know you are no such snake."

"Procurator, His Majesty wishes me to inform you of a matter much debated in the Senate, which concerns the punishment and death of Uriahkles."

"The tenth month from the insurgency has invited itself into oblivion, and now you have devised, no doubt, a death worthy of some great insult to me and my people. What is it?"

"You are to die in the Coliseum—"

Interrupting, Uriahkles observes, "You have conquered our country, slew our soldiers, raped our women, enslaved innocence, and sacrificed to your alien gods in the Holy of Holies, thus making the so-named sacrificer a mere butcher, an apocalypse to reason. The Coliseum was built on the backs of slaves, and to justice shall I say their names, declaring that they are children of the Chosen. I am to die where they died after their deaths. If it so pleases God, then may it be so."

Whereto the Senator replies, "You know where to take him. Let the Procurator continue in his bloodless ties to an alien people, thinking his death pleasure house to a more brutal god than our own. Jerusalem is sacked, and its citizens enslaved either as our servants or our whores, sometimes both as so you say," pausing, he wishes some opportunity to beget a despicable temperance; this done, he now resumes; "Gods who contract thus are no more gods than a thief hath riches." The guards join in the Senator's lingering laughter, after which Uriahkles is led away.

He's taken now to a pit in the Coliseum where hung various weapons and a few yet remaining scents of death's own stench. The awful clamour of the audience disturbs the soul, but superfluous martyrs may still find patience. Uriahkles is no different.

Soon, Caesar speaks, saying:

"What, now, shall we to justice if not for he who Rome has so worsened, made wretched, and most disagreeable? We have chosen a time for the traitor to die, and verily at the first does he now come to join us soon. Be patient, and wait for your deliverance up to the God to whom you pray now.

"Our father, the noble Caesar, trusted him most like a son, a man in whom the gods saw the prestige and the power of their worthiest subjects, the greatest conquerors. Was not he by our father's blessing made governor of that State most repulsive to Rome? Was not he guilty of betraying a father's love, and forsaking his kindred so kind to him for a condemned people, whom we know as the Jews, a race most disagreeable to the gods?" Titus pauses to bathe his ears with the kind reception of the crowds, all wanton enthusiasts to the onslaught coming on.

Titus resumes, "Since duty dictates the fate of such a man we have heartily brought him to you now as our own warning to the enemies of Rome."

With these pronouncements, a Praetorian signals Uriahkles leave, and thus the gates are thrown open, permitting the prisoner the great view of the amphitheatre. His entrance is welcomed by a brief silence soon torn to pieces by ensuing booing.

Four Praetorians stop some ten feet before him, staking their positions parallel to his station as does the last two, who now make opposite movement by advancing in the remaining direction.

Caesar gestures a signal to the guards, and a voice behind the helmet informs permission for Uriahkles to bid speak to the Emperor.

He doesn't, though.

"As thou art wordless, so too shall we make thee worldless," says the Emperor, after which the crowd gives great cheer. The time to enjoy their cries is done, allowing Caesar to continue; "For your crimes most grievous against the greatest of States, abominations too great to be remembered, I have bid the historians your eternal effacement from memory, you shall be put to death by order of the People of Rome. You shall die by being devoured by lions, and so it is that we have appointed you a new position worthy of your station in the society whom you did forsake for a foreign people. You are food for hungry beasts, just as you were once for the carnivorous Jews!" Great laughter, particularly frightening, follows this latest remark; Caesar is apt to extend his ridicule; "and this time there is no hope of making them herbivores by your betraying your allegiance. These beasts know of no other commitment than to their own bellies in all its various forms, sacrificing all reason." Stopping again, the laughter does, indeed, drown out any spectre of hope for the Hebrew People. *Rome will have to go, but when?*

Caesar shall sit now, but first his command to the slaves. "Release the beasts that they may know their kin."

At this, the Praetorians return to the dark of the dungeons; their absence is quickly replaced by the sound of different impatient predators. The crowd continues to clamour such that Olympus appears to quake at it.

Interruption.

A spectator leaps from the front row, his face frenzied with indifference, and makes stop atop the dust of the Coliseum. He makes his way before the box wherein sits the Emperor. He speaks directly to its occupant.

"Hail, Caesar! I beseech speech with Your Majesty."

Caesar, always contriving reality for appearance, sees a golden opportunity by reason of the suddenness, and so he humours the old man.

"What shall we talk about, Neptonius, father of Uriahkles?"

"Mercy, but mercy not of the art of blind love, but mercy of the truth of all-seeing Justice. By reason of this, do I now petition your attention, my lord."

"How," says Titus mockingly, "do you propose such a feat, considering the dread and circumstance of this your son's present hour?"

"By revealing the nature of the disease which made my son ill of all reason."

"Speak, then, for Caesar is turned to hear."

"Uriahkles is not the son of Romans, but of mixed union has he come, for his mother is a Jewess, and I her lover, together the proud parents of young Uriahkles here. My son never knew her for she died in childbirth, and I, not wishing to raise his heart half-drawn, took to wife a Roman in whom I saw qualities no different from Uriah's mother. His betrayal, then, is no more than the orphan in search of origins. Uriahkles has always been most drawn to his mother, and confided to me once that though he loved my new bride, he thought it exceptional how unlike in temperament they were. His heart knew homesickness before it knew the homeland. Soothsayers and auguries said as much, and warned still greater calamities for the son in whom the spirit of his people never abandoned, and whom I love more than I do Rome itself. Ask any Jew, my lord, and they shall tell you what now I say: it is by the mother that the Jew is made a Jew by reason of the blood bondage. And is not the father at fault in the failure of a son? Has not Rome made it such? My son is guilty but of one crime alone. I, on the other hand, am guilty with more crimes on my head than there are stars in Olympus or grains of sand with their presence gracing all great Neptune's beaches!"

Titus is amused, but provides Uriah's grieving father with further grief.

"Hear Neptonius, hear what now Caesar rules for your honour's sake, of which, we'll have it be known, some in the Senate say is as great as Brutus', you whom we bequeath now redemption may have our word of mercy to spare your son, this Jew, born of insurgent blood from foreign soils, this traitorous defiler of the laws of our fathers, but this, too, as it us befitted the nature of Rome, shall come with blood, with individual tears for some general epilogue.

"Your son shall have our leave to live, but you must die no different a death than he. Speak not, but, on our Honour, go speak to your son where none have ear than the Gods themselves, and there with tear and terror embrace him, for all in Rome had once had to share in your grief, making the great halls of governance and the ceaseless trampling feet atop roadways of commerce but a single note to be heard from your second wife's cheeks. Now we wish to end it and be done with all whom are deemed member of that insurgent, subservient race. Then with this for leave it'll be wise to go now, if Caesar's word yet has certain weight for your Atlas shoulders!"

Neptonius does not bow, but moves coolly on the stage like some ghost in the dark, haunting by reason of memory all that saw him thus. He is seen to his son, who waits for him by the entrance to the Coliseum proper. A group of strangers, numbering six, are also there.

Neptonius stares at his son, his pale constitution no less motionless than statues of cold childless Caesar. The consciousness of his position is shaken by what is being registered by vision, silent in expressing his compassion, as is the nature of a truant Stoic, a deluging sense of quiet disbelief mixes now with the bitterness of his tears, strolling down the cheeks. . . . tasting the paradoxes of a bewildering epoch. He embraces his son with the same kind of suddenness to which he submitted himself when he began building the altar on which he would sacrifice himself.

Holding on, he says, "Son, forgive me for not being a wiser father." Uriahkles cannot speak; grief refuses to allow him speech.

"Uriah?"

"Yes, father."

"Please allow me to do this, sickness took your mother away from us and grief took the women whom you called mother and now I am deserted. So great was the love she had for you—and she knew the secret,' he paused, attempting to steady his words; "May the God to whom you have pledged allegiance see to your safety from this time forth, Abram's God. Your mother told me a story about a Jew, the first Jew, whom you call Abraham. I know how according to Scripture God commanded him to sacrifice his son, Isaac, on Mount Moriah, and obeying him, having Isaac readied as sacrifice on the altar, raised his hand to kill Sarah's son. I, too, shall sacrifice, and not my son but myself. I do not expect an angel to intervene on behalf, considering how he didn't intervene in the destruction of Herod's temple or your people. I shall be still and allow my people to do their worst.

"Doctor? I believe you remember Eurythikles, my son?"

The doctor emerges, speaking sadly, "Hello, Uriah. Your father established word with Caesar, when your heroism was being lauded by Titus's father and during the course of his investigations, he happened upon my name. Formality soon over, I told him I would help you. I, too, made contact with a man, of whom you heard during your sojourn in the Orient, a name, which though anonymous, shall be the guardian of your name, being that Rome has now effaced it . . . Rabbi?"

A man stepped forth, introducing himself, "Shalom, Uriah."

Uriah remembered him well. "You are the one they call Sharhanim."

"I am, yes."

"Tell me, I knew you did tell your tales in such a place that I would surely hear them. But why did you seek to speak with me?"

"My father, Rabbi Avraham, heard about a woman who had been rescued by a Roman. Her mother told him about her daughter's affection for this man, and in turn heard about his affection for her. Her mother finally relented, and they were married in secret; my father blessed the marriage. Upon his death, he confided to me that a child had been born to them, but at a great cost: the loss of your mother. Neptonius remarried, but his new bride was barren, and so she raised you as her own. My father told me to look after you when the time came, believing you were a gift from God. I never broke my promise to my father."

Neptonius continued, saying to his son, "Together, you shall join them, the exiles. Rabbi Sharhanim shall take you to Hispania, where, perhaps, you'll be able to rebuild what has been razed to the dust."

"Now, my son, you shall go—and leave your fool-father to his fate."

• • • • • •

Disappearing into the distance, Uriah could hear nothing but the fading cries of an alien people, in whose loud and anonymous voice struck the memory with images of a stranger existence.

Perfect sorrow now mangles his mingled emotions, and the dawn has yet to be torn apart from its counterpart, dusk.

THE LOST WATCHTOWERS OF MARSAILLES

How now, the experiment of language?
Of all the scholars not one hath reason,
Though be this so, a few shall wisdom choose
To the bridle brain discern the deed I have done.
Thus hath relief indignant convocation.

THE ARCHITECT OF THE TOWER

Like as the wolves make towards wounded sheep, so too are the ruins haunted by silence.

Of all the ruins by which desire obtains consciousness of the ineffectual yesteryear, no one is so violent as the lost watchtowers of Marsailles. This is hardly offending to expectancy, especially when one sees for themselves how these injured antiquities, sad but sober witnesses, usually succeed in having the sharp sense riddled. So sharp has stung their stranger sadness that the faculty of good sense, whereon temperate dispositions sadly rely, lies seduced with no means of redemption, the faculty is thus forsaken. Though their inspection is a crucible, the unusual quality to which consciousness has attached the solitude of the antique shrine is disturbingly affable. The time-devoured battlements appear even primeval in their uncanny ability to illicit fear and faith, anger and anxiety, irreparable happiness.

Two hooded figures appear conjoined to the chaos, black shadows attempting to court the wind as their featureless garments do frenzy with stillness. The grey, darkening complexion with which the sky has decorated itself is befitting the gloomy movements of these men: Dark Age wanderers. Sombre men, thin and either of average height, with a most indistinct impression of devastation defining their reticent eyes; and yet these olive-skinned passers-by, despite this violent despondency, are quick to quiet the mind in order to meditate upon the bitter solace of the shrine. Their faces are barely visible, their voices hardly audible. They appear to whisper amongst themselves.

"Tell me, Manasseh, what knowledge captured, have the masters of Marsailles, for can it be that what has happened can regain knowledge, so as to deprive the privilege of what is known that it makes room for action to have done what has now been undone and unknowingly?" asks a voice considerate in its nature, with full awareness and the weight of astonishment in observing the violence of the vestiges.

"Yes, Shoach," his companion replies; "neither the conqueror nor the conquered have secured either triumph or tragedy."

The lonely passers-by are possessed by what they see. They appear enraptured like humble pilgrims by the epiphany in Renaissance artwork–be it whichever representation–to each facial expression an observer would deem fit an eternity of description, a scholar an infinity into which to throw the time required to complete manuscripts for such an onerous task.

"I have heard of this monastery in my journeys. Was it not in before-times a castle?"

"Yes, it was," replies he.

Their curiosity segregates them from indifferent appearance, but what has begun, as fascination, shall shortly become convincement. The silence is sedentary.

Manasseh begins to recount its history, explaining:

"The castle was abandoned by its pagan occupants, but soon transformed by Christian ambition into a monastic institution. Monks hid here, not knowing what suddenness does when it happens upon such hiddenness. The bureaucratic nest they formed was inconstant to the vision established by its chief administrators, and being too concerned with scruples, they were orphaned to oblivion when Vandals sacked the monastery, reducing its celebrated contents to pure legend. What, now, was to become of the building, this attractive abode which refused to vanish into misty veils, and yearned to be rebuilt?

"Among the dead there was a survivor, a monk in whom fate saw an obscure opportunity to preserve certain eccentricities of nature which, though sinister and mysterious, captured the unlikely providence which befell Marsailles. His name has been forgotten, but history appears to relish the fact that his account, concerning what came to pass following the success of the siege, has survived when its author, though spared by accident during the assault, could not find like patronage against forgetfulness during the equally barbarous siege of Chronus, which is nature's profane conflagration.

"His chronicles have as their principal concern the considerable extent to which the Vandals became dazzled by Marsailles' crushing pride and appalling complexity. Unable to lute her with an indifferent conscience, disarmed by grandeur and silence, the barbarians began to entertain the notion of abandoning their spoil, and setting forth deeper into the wilderness.

"He describes with growing astonishment the irregular esteem, without which the barbarians would not have been able to examine the immense complex; a miraculous feature to be observed, says he, since they had begun with careless sessions, of which I interpret to signify inconstant stares at Marsailles' attractive architectural integrity.

"When the night was old he reports having perceived emotions of unusual disposition beginning to assume residence in the intemperate hearts of Marsailles' new lords. Originally the disturbing paradigm of pagan hedonism, these savage soldiers had now begun to indicate a declining fervour in their pursuit of pleasuring the senses. And continuing his observation of their cooling passion for chaos, owing to a certain propensity in subtlety, what had happened to the Vandals was–so he solemnly testifies–the most miraculous, monotonous wonder he had yet known or was capable of imagining. I argue that this is uncanny nature brought to perfection: a controversial chronicle.

"This minister was trained in the faith of his father in order to have promulgated their convocation and conviction. The salvation of souls and the gift of knowledge of the Saviour was his purpose. He was, therefore, an agent of Christian conversion, itself an agency which, if nature provided a prudent propensity, would have surely been punctilious in posture and prose. We know that he did commit to excellence a discerning toleration for the magic arts, and as for the religion, of which I know to be equally built upon miracle as it is on sermon—it requires the mind to be accustomed, as for example, in envisaging similitudes of a most striking disposition; and in being so made, these images are either of exceptional beauty or singular ugliness: gruesome, grotesque ingenuities made with the intent of advancement towards the sublime.

"He most certainly would have found it an accustomed practice to deal with such matters as angels, demons, sins, senses, miracles, damnations, the passion, and the like deliverance and apocalyptic prophecy, so as to multiply sadly the hard fate upon which he nearly came to approximate Spartacus'. Yet he did with a keen and discerning faculty no less brazenly declared himself beholden of a spectacle to which the calm sweet terribleness of the race's history appears insubstantial and illogical, further alleging in his report how of all the scenes he yet had seen, this was the more pressing and imperfect, a mythological grandeur against which no competition is successful."

The report fuelled his companion's memory, no less so than his imagination. Shoach comments, saying, "Yes, I appear to recall a passage of his now:

'The silence of Marsailles is–so I have observed–the most ingenious device yet conceived by the inventors in order to combat the inglorious proposition which I have heard thus expressed: "Ignorance is innocence."'

"The citation is audacious, sacrilegious—the ravings of a desperate mind. Such interpretations are not, however, appropriate in description to the minister's chronicle, especially given the quality of what came to pass."

To which Manasseh replies, 'Indeed,' after which he continues to recount.

"With the first half of the fortnight gone, the minister qualified his astonishment.

"Concealing his presence in a variety of locations, he saw the abundance, the mindmangled enjoyments and pastimes of his unwitting captors. He writes of their excessive consumption of drink, continuous orgies, gladiatorial spectacles, maltreatment of inferiors, and flagrant disregard for anything just and respectable. Their feasts are feats of demonic indulgence, and do not merit the title of banquet but butchery, says he. They seem to secure pleasure in belching noxious vapours, and doing violence to the serenity of God's earthly kingdom. The wolves may not howl worse, nor the bear appear more grisly when these savages take to disturbing the air with their vociferous articulations, and parading around the castle confines in their animal skins; they do assume in absence to imperfection the guise of damned spirits. He continues to chronicle in this vein, for quite some time, until something wondrous presents itself, comes to attention.

"Having taken shelter in the library, he is struck to see a barbarian committing wondrous acts of originality. The development of the unlikely became likely when he saw Vandals trying to read the books."

"Certainly—What is this miracle?" asks Shoach, interrupting the report.

"Good Shoach, it is, as they say, only the beginning. For the minister proceeds to chronicle, in cataloguing the register of that which comes to pass; he appears to abandon his faith."

"What? What have the events detailed, good my Manasseh?"

"What remains of the account, unfortunately, are fragments, detailing not specifics but riddles, almost. The last paragraph records how his captors found him, apologizing for their crimes, and begging him for forgiveness. They couldn't speak to him, owing to the fact that their language was foreign, but did prostrate themselves in such a way as to make apparent what it was they couldn't begin to articulate. Setting out to remedy this, the minister then instructs them in Latin, the details of which are lost but they're soon fully capable of speaking to one another. The instructions over, they leave Marsailles together, after burying and mourning the dead for six days and nights. The chronicle concludes with an inconclusive remark."

"Who built the fortress?" asks Shoach, his fading whispervoice clearly expressing his dying scepticism and burgeoning fascination with Manasseh's retelling of the minister's account.

"It was built by Jewish slaves under the administration of Rome."

"What was its purpose?"

"Vulgar, most likely; that is, until the revolt. The slaves rebelled against their masters, and secured their freedom when they had expulsed the yoke of tyranny from off their backs. The triumph, however, was short-lived; and returning with a considerable force, the Romans defeated the Jews during the siege, and adjudicated them the dishonoured guests of misty-eyed Pluto. How it sometimes pleases the deity to provide hope when hope seems all but irrational! For you see, as was the case with barbarians, so too did history fall upon itself by marrying irony to inevitability."

"You mean, good Manasseh, there was a survivor?"

"Yes."

"What is his name?"

"His name, Shoach, was Tolocusah Ben Lishkotev."

"Did he too leave an opus for posterity?"

"It has, alas, come down to us only in fragments. Time has left us these arresting passages, which he wrote before abandoning Marsailles:

'The silence eloquently describes the scenery. I cannot hear the stone flung into the water, but I think myself audience by reason of the ear to the ripples thereby produced. I am blind to the flying birds, but I know myself to be of audience, by reason of the eye, to their freedom. My hands are sensitive to what I see, and my eyes to what I touch. I am quiescent when darkness fell that evening, but whether I am asleep or awake, experiencing or imagining, be it either which, my faculties do not falter, and so provide me with an endless degree of energy the exact extent to which they rose, I am unable to describe. I cannot capture the scent of the pine tree, but I imagine myself partaking the perfume of their roots, which lay deep beneath the soil, as by reason of the appropriate gatekeeper. I am denied the presence of my people, but yet I remain conscious of their consciousness, just as the migrating fowl, being children of a constant exodus, continue such like awareness to the cycles of nature. My tongue is responsive to what I smell, and my nose to what I taste. I reside in stillness, and it beautifully rebukes the rancour of certain superfluous movements.

'There is no need for reciprocal pretence here; necessity became indifferent to nature, and nature reconcilable with the imagination.

'The chattering of wind and voices, thus the last soul of Rome, has vanished from my stream of discernment, which has emptied itself into redoubtable preservation. I am alone, but the breaking of wood against rock appears to keep me company. Truth was near where I was then, as by interruption. The means with which I was concerned did never concern me so. The abilities of an anfractuous gesture–the necessary foundation–the arbitrary jest, a mixed madness, it is redundant and lays refuted. How I am part of the indestructibly inexorable, of which makes itself an indelible part of the frame of the world. I did not escape the thick taste of wretchedness, but merely have returned to my previous state of regiment.

'The course of thought is mapmaking, not the search for the mapmaker, between which to draw difference is to draw interference. Nature is my nature. The significant difference being that unlike the celestial ceiling, I am apt to multiply not with myself at war. I pay not for peace by entertaining notions of conquest, when was military operations ever waged at an affordable rate! Does this not mean that I would have to vacant a public execution house? I came to later describe it,' unfortunately this passage has been lost to us, but what remains I'll recite now; 'this was the calm after the storm. Fidgeting fixtures are still as statuary, the snide of smiling murderers have been swallowed up by nature, and gaping within myself I see who I once was depart from me. Sullen, trussed to truth, waxed indignant at Protean corruption, nativity, the Romans who I survived did not survive themselves and being mad, they fell upon their own swords and I buried them.'

"But tell me, good Manasseh; is his vision, too, a stranger to your eyes?"

"I may if we, too, survive ourselves."

"The surviving reports are unique, Manasseh, in their unanimous verdict concerning the castle's apparent ability to instruct its inhabitants in the way of accepting perfection. It defined for the Romans the savage species of their paradox, forcing their hand to enact violence against themselves.

"The survivor," says Manasseh, "one of our ancestors, was reported to have been the son of a mystic, a man initiated into the deeper mysteries of the faith. He was not a mystic himself, however, and so I am sceptical and confident in refusing to let superstition take hold of my desire to find the truth."

"What became of the Jew?"

Manasseh replies calmly now, as if whispering has taken hold of his tongue; "He vanished, and was never heard from again."

"What news more does the chronicle defend?" asks Shoach, impelled deeply now.

"With the Romans buried, he provides us the following esoteric proclamation: "Eternity shall abandon to reside in the question, and orphaned itself to the answer. Marsailles is the parent of the process." [This passage, against intuition, discretion and experience, must remain riddled with what I am only able to describe as thick-ripped complexity: no simplicity is to be in any way allowed here.]

"What do you think happened to him?"

"He did not abandon Marsailles, at least I do not think so. My suspicion is adamant in thinking that he came and went as he pleased, travelling to a few of the neighbouring villages in order to impress upon them his message of hope for God's chosen people. For you see, the villages which are near Marsailles are all Jewish, populated by the children of the Diaspora."

"And what, he who knows, is this message of hope of which he spoke?"

"Well, my good Shoach, legends abound and seem to provide comfort for the impoverished, but the tales I have been told are united in their grudging consensus concerning his message's apparent disregard for war, and worship."

"How mean you so?"

"In this regard I shall do justice to your question by recounting one of these anecdotal histories. The author's anonymous, Shoach, so you need not ask the question. As for their preservation, the writings have come down to us by reason of monastic clerics, all of whom are united in impressing upon the reader an urgent caution in reading them. I'll recount an account of common variety, which is in verse, and some good length too:

'Shall I tell thee how thy fairest features
Do violence and more virtue than all the gods,

Mine, or thine; heavenly, or earthly? O, sweet wonder!
Whom I have so long missed, *make me mortal with a kiss*.
For thy lips are but key to unlocking all mystery,
"Tis the Mind's longing for grace,
Far greater than the sea's embrace;
The arrow of Cupid hath struck my heart!
Blinding all other minor beauties,
Either of wretched Venus, or imperfect Psyche;
Binding me to the beauty, which hath no other.
May mine eyes glimpse thee most glorious sight
By all visions thereof counselled. Oh, dove,
Whose wings and melodies
Are far more faithful than unfaithful love,
Than cupid himself!
Thou hast struck my heart's
Grandest grace and left it in solitude,
Sans thee I am but to nourish upon
The shadow of complexion of that which thou art.
O, most immortal star, give me thy true heart,
For I am no truant to God's subtle design, nay!
Of the fabric and the solace—
As I came upon a meadow I saw,
Near some farmer's field, this little cottage of old,
Crowned with soil that even now doth draw
Me with lightest touch a gentle solace.
Thus with the great passion, which so I grew,
That I, with thoughts swift as love or hatred,
Could not bounded be but to construe
Whose beggar-like feet doth with ache tread
Upon the finely cut and woven wood
Of this most serene, calm, and sad-like place.
So I got me near the window and there stood
With amazement struck; how the sleepy space
Was filled with a young maiden whose mild breath
Was soft by lace making until her gentle death.'

"Here's another, much in the same vein:

'No grand fleet did the Corinthians claim,
Yet discerning Sisyphus, he who was,
Be the proclamations of chroniclers,
The monarch most royal of deep mischief
To ever have governed upon the throne;
He who had sent–now we know–soldiers,
Be they of the most mercenary mangled minds,
To find sleep's brother atop foreign soils,
Did soberly elect to embark upon the
Corinthian fleet's sagacious construction.

How he, impish and most keen of all knaves,
Did accomplish the sudden desire
Remaineth hidden from all history;
'Tis lost being there strictly then consigned
To the abyss of men's minds, thus only in
The unmeasured depths of undiscovered dreams
Is all art capable to contemplate how
He, of uncertain thought, did manage certainty
Most grievous.

The great military gift slept at quiet seas,
But the Corinthian port principally.
Yet what in reason hath most righteous-endured
The torture of the turning of the clock
Is that Sisyphus dared to have dreamt a dream
Greater than any vision of the gods:
An epiphany heretofore novel!

Waking eternally from eternal sleep,
Heralding thus the death of Death itself.

All stars are drunk deep by Olympus' fire.
To their wild but majestic world

Be there found immortal intoxication,
So too was King Sisyphus by his love.
She was his immortal soul, and he hers.
Love for them was
An indefinite inebriation,
The means whereby ancient age fell obsolete,
And bequeathed boundless bliss the heart's hunger.

Verily at the first did they love;
Sufficient unto the truth was their vision thereof.
What greater proof wherewith to pledge sacred vows?
But if love was their corporal unity,

Mischief had been their spirituality.
For verily at the first did they know
Mischief came as interminable lifeblood.

When many years of faithful rule had passed, Sisyphus vowed to bequeath greater devotion to the Queen, that he might tell Her Majesty how was it when they first embraced, kissed, loved:

To which cheek was the dear imprint made?

Assuming residence in their banquet hall, Her Majesty upon the throne with eager audience, this being all herself, Sisyphus stands

To tell how it was when they were lovers:

Our hearts, weak and weary as be they so,
Have in their beating the bleeding of woe.
Like as some glass fractured by hardened rocks,
So too did breathing offend uninspired lungs.
Each word–methinks–natured dishonest tongues.
What profit, then, the crowing of the cocks?
Why not sleep to dream the idle king away,
Professing ignorance to dallied days?

The looking glass, against the inventors,
Did dispel melancholy's conventors,
Not orderly reflecting the face's truant class.
Thus bewitching the brain impertinent brass.
But if felicity permit me to contemplate thee
Thou, my immortal love, be mine eyes to see.
I by need am charged to renew the mind,
So in thy keen memory mayest thou find
The sweet silent remembrance of old love.
I ask the gentle goddess of the dove
To support me in this grievous pursuit
Thus by reason of the passion's lawsuit,
Wherewith captivity teaches thee to crave,
As thou, in thyself, binds thee thine own slave,
So too like the cruel gluttony of Death
Is life devoid of thy sweet rosy breath.
So with seeming sorrow in an idle tear,
Is now the image received from old-world mirrors past
When new envious findest thou thy face aghast.
We be so to delight ourselves to quickly find
How it goes when hearest thou love did but bind
Once on a time, as old men say of us,
How I alone did thee see by love's dust
The mortal instrument with whom sadness flees,
And the little love-rogue his mischief glees.
But wake these quests!
I have no requests.
Dear life, I break thee off!
O, my dearest love! Thee shall I see anon,
When some chronicle perchance shall sing our song.'

"Death tapped the king's shoulder, and yet a few fears did frenzy eternity. For Savvy Sisyphus went on to do a noble number of the most mischievous deeds the mind of men has yet achieved, fooling death and deceiving the gods, making the immortals out to be, well, mortal.

"Hades came to collect him, bringing along with him a pair of handcuffs, this being somewhat of a novelty; and Sisyphus naturally impressed upon the dark lord his interest in the device. He requested a demonstration of their use, and his persuasion being an image of perfection—for truly that was what it was—Hades complied by handcuffing himself down in one of the King's dungeons. Sisyphus then stuck him in a closet, some miscellaneous place in the palace, and by doing so effectively ending the reign of death itself.

"The gods intervened, and though death returned, with harsh-hearted Hades summarily ordering Sisyphus to register himself, to resign to his eternal consignment, he had yet within himself more mischief with which to blind those who've learned how to see what is not in front of their eyes.

"He hadn't been buried, telling his wife to do as much, and so having certain unalienable arguments, all of which he brought to Persephone, complaining how he hadn't been given those obsequies and funeral honours rightfully due to a king. This wasn't the only piece to his puzzle, however; for being an unburied corpse, he had no right to dwell in the land of the dead. "Do I not have," he asked, "no coin in the mouth, nothing under the tongue? How was I to be found on the far side of Styx if I hadn't paid that old Ferryman his due? Need I not to ask that Her Highness sees most certainly how things are all amiss, and that I must be granted leave to come back topside, to give order justice, is only just, and most necessary.

"The knave had his way, he who had moit rather than imperfected an imprecise art of mixing mischief with persuasion, and his absence from death lasted for yet another good plot of time. The beginning must have its end, and so Sisyphus was returned again to death, charged with crimes against the gods. His eternal prison term was to roll a heavy stone to the top of a hill, and yet having done the deed for which he was destined to always do, the object of his torment rolled back down again, and this vicious cycle of calculated agony was ceaseless, never ending, and final: a last testament. And so it is said that this palace, Marsailles, was once the ground on which he had built his own, the very place where death had died."

Steadying his words, the minstrel resumes to tell another tale, "Such action brings to mind Icarus, son of Daedalus, who escaping with his father from Crete came to learn the terrors of truth, of how dark may be found in light. For flying with wings made of wax did he ascend, ascending so high that the sun's heat grew hungrier, devouring the material by which hope had been fastened. The outcome became inevitable, sending him into death's waiting arms. One of our minstrels puts it thus:

'Dark, cold: damp.
The labyrinth is created,
There are scores of cul-de-sacs and tortuous passage-ways,
Snaking across the obscure region to which they have been assigned.
The metal tributary is serene and
Can be heard as softest whispers, as
From an orchestra of secret lovers,
Which like leaves
Blown from off their departed station,
Are being heard like a hundred
Sacrifices, through obscure incantations,
Into the dark places of the undesired.
The sanctuary, quiet like a graveyard,
Continues to impress upon me–so I should abbreviate–
The savage uncertainty of which I constantly remain conscious,
Whether I am asleep or awake.
In the distance, as a thought
Is to the human mind,

A melancholy truth is in song.
I appear to sing of possessions, precious possessions;
These all appear to have been taken away from us quite some time ago,
I'm afraid.
The sad spectre is pure yellow, as
Gold.
I find myself unable to contemplate its finer features of form,
Lost, as ancient sages say, by the angry consciousness of an inattentive mind.
The face is an image of imperfection,
The lost love of a previous existence, to which now I am all but oblivious.
Its voice is pleasing to listen to,
The rare quality of a full and forbidding moon.
The hands are hardened, black like some old miner's,
Insensitive to the incuriosity of material sense—
Nature appears to provide the presence of patronage,
Thus supplying the dictatorial requirements of a raging creativity.
Its size, shape, and substance are images
Of seeming, all-devouring perfection
Itself.
In the unclear distance,
The truth is running away, away from me.
Its every inch of constitution,
Whether bone, or breath; the invisible, or the apparent;
Appears to muster all its strength in order to escape from me.
The company most desired,
Truth,
Is afraid of its most ardent seeker,
For I am the inhabitant of such an occupation;
I cannot resist the impulse to discover,

To disregard opinion, and disadvantage myself too many.
This aspect of faith flows through the body,
Intoxicating ignorance, but engendering the means to combat it.
It is a dire blood, which being a thing of necessity,
Stings the heart with a
Different kind of
Priority. Probity remains indifferent, however
In a thousand myths
He desires to tell you the truth,
Nature must have the means with which to understand the imagination,
No differently than the imagination must too have those same means
With which to contemplate and comprehend nature.
Mythology is a hunter that I think
Does well to apprehend earth by reason of the enigma.
The present moment unravels itself,
Swift in its dissolution,
What experience registers is what imagination redesigns,
Memories reconstruct, but fancies resurrect.
The action is charged as thunderous disturbance to an act of
Consciousness,
Desperation adopts the orphan, and being Herod-like,
Discharges slaughtermen to make nature its equal,
Thus bequeathing his most treasured possession, which is the legitimate father of all invention.
Death stretches ever so far out
His arms, his hands, his body, his awareness —
About to seize life eternally,
The widow and the orphan turn to a tuft of needs
In a manner which, though virtuous to a fault, echoes

The suddenness of nature, the demonic spontaneity of constant reinvention, a disgraceful trust in the uncertain.
I observe with a keen and indistinct eye
How Marsailles quickly dissolves itself into a fledging forgetfulness.
And this has made, gradually but naturally,
The impression of magic conjuring, sombre incantation,
Christian ideology, which to the Jew is an embarrassment of excessive flattery;
Haven't their persecutors discerned wise Abraham, his universal testament to his God, whose hatred of idolatry is surpassed only by his passion?
The watchtowers are watching me, more than I am watching the stars.
A cartographer's atlas,
Which is made of memory
And the war against which he fought, until peace pieced itself back together again.
The silence is auspicious, but not suspicious of a particular position of consciousness.
And thus I have with a keen, though yet silent, mind
Contemplated the fragile whispers of her soulless cries.
It is the testament he knows as he dies.
This is the inauspicious expulsion, thinking,
Committing to action the text of immortal thought.
Marsailles' architecture is the phoenix of antiquity,
Which is frozen not in hallow hymns of illegitimate piety,
But in the material maternity of alabaster stone: concrete epiphany.
Observing its medieval edifice has my sin burned and purged away.
The ashes of previous enchantment,
An inflamed brain of combustion, a

Thought, is soon subsumed by roaring expectation.
Oh, why do I have this tongue with which to language my languished estate?
Wherefore existence?
If 'tis but to maim and mash crippled sheep!
What will to wound he who hath the potent
Faculty of a maternal womb with child,
Weaker wrecks: sophomoric stoics all!
The mere sight of me sends them fleeing hence,
In the frenzied state of imperious fear,
As if I am a thousand wolf-faced, a dread disease, unholy fear.
Am I defended by the cries of terror and desire?
With the means only to send the sheep weeping
Wolf!
Forgetfulness, obscurity: nothingness.
I am he who says I am, but who are they?
They are children of foolish fate, discipled to
Fickle fashion, false faces, and fantastic frenzies?
I in an imposed servitude am,
Justice and Rightness shall send me thither.
What is the potency of prophecy?
What are the plagues of international passion?
To death shall I defend the last contemplative organism?
Standing, living, breathing: existing.
Stillness moulds the movement of the hands,
The thrusting wind is swift in its arrest,
But far gone are the winds of adversity.
They've been blown into the womb of oblivion.
Grey
Clouds do mutually draw into a flower long
The fresh lustre of incandescent spring,
Whose sacred dimension is as far as no longing can reach.
It is where the great Beggar be, Truth.
For now adversity mourns for its Kingdom of Sand.

The vaporous metropolis of your madness,
The dim deed of grace has fall'n from my hand,
Thus adopting the Empire of Flown.
Love ascends the celestial influences,
And so begins the metamorphosis, a flight, greater than
Day or night.
The leader of the Way Finders is in sight,
Eternity bids them welcome.
O, beggar, let me see what thee unites,
That I may from thee discern the sacred urn,
Thus crushing all oblivion with godly pride.
Now truth profounder than the sea hath grown,
Permitting thy patron to glimpse thy immortal face.
The old muse hath he whom now I know not,
Among a brave but wounded vessel sits he,
Steadfast by reason of the silence hath night
Seen Daedalus, the inventor.
        Methinks
Like as the full and florescent moon is he,
And so stands the sombre shade of new Samos,
This primal progeny of sweet Aurora's kiss.
For in the dark do I see him bathing,
Entertaining incessant paradoxes,
Like some ghost new-haunted of sulphurous mansion.
Likeness is his crown, as does the moon claim.
        What centrepiece more than the great son in whom
        Daedalus in reason hath purpose found.
So he sheds the dark to bleed its bounty,
To yield the harvest of bounteous mystery,
Thus relinquishing God's sober secrets.
The mouth of black night is stubborn,
And the prince of puzzles does now with his son contend
The boundless regions of great Prometheus;
He who gave man the first mysticism,

This thing called fire, which by another
Appellation is christened the Christ.
Daedalus along with his son Icarus
Do now with majestic anger suffer
The damnation of Father's inventions,
Which the ancients did assign the title Labyrinth.
The wrath of Jove's haughty son have they incurred,
Disobedience most intolerable
Have by royal order been thrown thither;
Like as slain fish tossed in merciless nets
Shall we now apprehend father and son.
The tangled, hauntingly tortuous construction,
        Whereinto thou, Minos, hast thyself thrown,
        Whom Minotaur thou callest thyself,
There held with its strong and savage spirit
Shalt thou Daedalus, the architect, findest.
'Tis strange–so methinks–how wheel and axle,
With each being accordant to nature,
Hath with a sad and inauspicious fate
Taken, I say, Time to be thy coffin,
Selfish Memory thy burial shroud.
The prison is now the house of the prisoner,
Daedalus, thou inventor, didst conceive,
Proscribe and manufacture its industry.
Why such madness to be thy weaponry
When art thou thyself he whom thou knowest not?
Against thee what art thy contraptions?
He who knows not now finds himself helpless.
Daedalus, a vessel whereto the tide of thought is unkind,
Apprehends in manners sudden certain
Possibilities, which, though obscure and ancient,
Washes ashore the impatient creativity
Whereof he knows to express, as nature doth
When she herself perfects her art to extremes.
Thus shall he like formulate, observing:
There's no maze I think more tortuous than myself.

Perchance to escape is the greater, my son.
Mark thou my words, unless the universe be thy kin:
Escape has its obscure ends at the crossroads,
Between which lies no distinction for land or sea,
But air alone are we free to wander.
As night fades away, Daedalus and Icarus escape the maze, having been so adopted by the ethereal ceiling.
With the abomination scarred by distance,
A memory,
The boundlessness of predawn air,
Icarus apprehends himself; his identity is his slavery.
The sober revelation has caused him
To be ferreted to a kingdom of self-appointed frenzy.
Liberty and tyranny are distant cousins which, though
Freedom he has secured from
The face of the monster, which he did not see, remains to
Remind him of what he spent lifetimes rubbishing.
Fear alone is the form of the menace, faith as fear.
Freedom, so thinks the inventor's son, is the subsistence, which alone binds the wings.
The ingredient has waxed forgetfulness in the mind of its consumer.
The winged angels
Ascend finally into the safest regions,
Spectators at the level of the dirt do think
They are witnesses to the soaring flight of gods.
Out of Crete and over the vastness of the sea
Is where the winged angels give flight now;
Birds freed from out of their cage,
Space regained,
Not by a material key, but by an impatient mind.
Icarus flies lightly, as a feather
When it falls from familiarity and is indifferently welcomed by its adoptive floor.

With no effort but will, undifferentiated will, does
Icarus provides numerous gaping wounds for the sky,
Soaring higher above than Babel.
Desperate Icarus, wiser than his father,
Thus begins to soar at a distance most strange and prudent.
Daedalus does not drop a sweat of doubt,
Discerning in his son's precocious desire
To wed necessity with creativity.
Danger appears not to be hunting them, he thinks.
With an army of furious thought, filling
His mind much like a crown adorns the head. Icarus
With an ever consuming contemplation,
An intelligent constitution of flesh and soul,
Faith and
Reason,
Sees suddenly the futility of his survival.
He is steadfast in his belief that they have not escaped.
Nor will they or anyone else ever escape from
The reconstruction of the previous abomination,
The monument his father subsequently bequeathed to madness.
The ubiquitous contraption haunts him,
He sees it's everywhere, and yet as he sees it, soars away from it,
Faster and faster, inexorable escape,
He's perceiving not what he's actually misperceiving, but by reason of the sense, at least so think the scholars, conceiving.
The perception with which he apprehends the maze is overwhelming;
Its design, colour and dimension overwhelm his imagination, but not his intellect, thus inviting a presence into possibility.
The emptiness of its void avoids him.

As he is about to touch the face of freedom, truth, and love, these being things of the earth,
The stubborn wax with which the wings are held,
Hold in place, as so to permit him the continuity of possibility, allowing him to escape from which place he knows not, have now begun to melt and give way
To the heat of the unforgiving sun,
The wings lose their strength, and the inevitable ensures: dissolution and insurgent acquiescence.
That he is falling unto the abyss, the murky deep of the sea; he has no doubt whatsoever about that.
He appears to welcome his fate.
His father races after him with a quick and ready faculty,
Too late: the mind that has looked upon the thought, regardless of humility, may not deny its truth.
Perception is deception, so he said once to his father.
What now the promised end of what is of the end?
Steadfast descending upon the deep waters,
Quiet streams of immeasurable profundity,
Icarus assumes a nonchalant consciousness,
A falling and frightful eclipse of the sun and moon,
By means of the memory which may so alleviate him,
So as to establish the grind of inconvalescent dispositions.
Sinking, being swallowed up
In accordance to the abysm's nature,
His last thoughts establish themselves by order
Of an unforgotten episode of childhood folly:

O, father, wherefore hast thou construed what
Thine enemies have christened the abomination?
Sufficient unto thy folly is the frenzy thereof.
What hast thou done?
Is death thy truant patronage?
What needs be thy birth but thy death?

Consumed
Hast thou been by the monsters of thine appetite.
Sorrow is thy sovereign, folly thy idolatry.
But be thou patient for what deeds thou hast done,
Discern thee thy immortal toil for thou,
Father, hast in thine intention slain thyself.

Icarus struggles against the waters, begins to drown,
suffocates and dies as his eyes refuse separation from
their father's.
Daedalus clamours the calm, and
Falls on the same sword on which his son fell,
Lands face first into the flood, drowns and dies.
The edge of its severing blade, slits the victim as it
slowly
Vanishes beneath death-punctuated flesh.
Here is where the angels are buried as with their commander.
Marsailles, though now on land, was once buried
Deep beneath the belly of Leviathan's kingdom.'

"It is, late, Manasseh; we must go," says Shoach; who quietly observes the remark; then is moved to tell more than what has been told, "The arrow of contemplation cannot miss the mark, and now I know I am in Marsailles. But there's another story, which quite hopeless in of itself, affords us the certainty of historic bankruptcies: a tower whose builders spoke with one tongue, the tip teaching how the untouchable was to be touched."

"I trust, Shoach, you mean—"

"Yes, the Tower of Babel," interjects he.

"Do you remember the story, Manasseh, about the Tower built in Babel?"

"I do, at least that's what my memory tells me."

"What, then, are you able to recollect?"

"The whole, and its parts."

"Tell me the story, then, that I may better understand what it is that you seek to reveal to me."

"I shall speak, then, of the people of whom you and I are part, calling to mind how nature, sick with ague and avengement, diseased with the angry god; his hungry servants, had now heralded for the construction of the consummate paradise: Babel.

"Noah's drunkenness echoed the vein of his sons' future vanity. Those who the Deluge had not taken began to take refuge in a desire to return to reality: Eden. Migrating from the east, they came upon a valley in the land whose name I have forgotten, and settled there where memory was abundant.

"They took various building materials, such as bricks, stone, bitumen and mortar, and began building for themselves a great tower with its tip in the heaven, in order to make a name for posterity; else they shall be still drowned by worse waters.

"I think it ironic how their index of labours, all of which are commonly held, perfectly embraced the imprudent and undisciplined characters of the account, the matter at hand. For they began building in order to be saved from the exile, only to be charged by God in grievance of their attempts to prevent this, an exile worthy of their original fears; the human figure at any given time casts shadows and reflections, thus he has made for himself many other selves, Babel being its uncanny manifestation.

"And so the God of the orphans came down, and passed judgment, banishing them. The tower's shadow was the length of a six-day journey, from east to west, and south to north, the sacred structure rose to dimensions equalled in height by the Tree of Knowledge of Good and Bad.

"I tell you, my good Shoach, my only friend, there was a man whose eyes last saw what it was that had been built. He said:

"I have been left much amazed, humbled, enlivened, and humiliated.

"The consequence was hideous . . . the columns are forsaken fruits:

'And he with valour of his craft did brave
For God came down to dig the human grave.
How now, the experiment of language?
Of all the scholars not one hath reason,
Though be this so, a few shall wisdom choose
To the bridle brain discern the deed I have done.
Thus hath relief indignant convocation.
Time shall not age nor space limit the monument
Which I with a keen and discernable
Eye have made in the dread image of thee, thyself.
May the times not forget he who hath battled
Ignorance, and came up himself no truant
To great Wisdom's sweet salient sessions.
Is God's spirit the language whereof thou speakest?'"

"Manasseh, I think I know what believe you now."

"What is it, Shoach?"

"Marsailles is to truth what Babel was to language."

MARACELSUS

The desperate heart tends to enslave the imagination so that it is capable of moulding all concepts in its image; its intention is to turn the base metal of an illusion into the pure gold of truth, a matter of fact.

THE COMPOSER OF “RIPARIAN EMPEROR”

The quiet waters seem to have been destined to continue this graceful guise, to which the observant eye–so it would struck–consigns an indifferent disposition towards disturbance, whether from nature or invention; be it either which, thus bemusing to its accustomed recourse that it promulgates repose, an offence to its previous histories.

The distant spectator, mysterious in his astute observations, is unsettled by the fickle charm of the river, of how composed he has found the monster. His bemusement is swift-footed to remind him of yet how abused the riverbank became, the once thin stomach of the sight, obese now, the extent of exhaustion to which just how it had become, with debris on account of the violent conversion of its companion, when nature, hastened by suddenness, evolved from ecstatic order to demonic chaos; and bearing witness to it, the mind refused to relinquish the image in order to entertain the almost absurd notion of its present disposition. "Ridiculous!" rises up an exclamation into the quiet air.

Change is inescapable, a commonly held belief by the sagacious—is simple enough to grasp in banquet conversations—but to make the instruction healthier by referring to experience, rather than idle adages, is to suspend rational prejudice for irrational reluctance. When confirmation came of unavoidable change, as if to knock on the door of incredulity, the youth remained in disbelief of the maxim; his violent revelation of commonsense seemed too much to bear.

"Is this kind creature that same ugly beast?" he asks himself; the tone quite hushed, though yet far from being hurried, as if to conceal a hideous deed, which now was irrecoverable. The reticent observer of the river gives himself over to meditation, after which he quietly returns to his dormitory, profoundly disturbed.

Young Maracelsus, a student of Enlightenment Viennese politics, has been reproached by experiment. He now elects to advance his studies by enrolling himself as a student of the arts.

Music.

This decision may bring him peace, but the fruit of his future labours shall bring him closer to anything but peace, or, at the very least, the peace to which we have attached all our confused sentimental notions. His is harmonious, and it may take the form of either the orderly or the chaotic, between which true harmony does not indulge with distinction.

Musical composition requires passion, such a dangerous and an irrational species thereof as if to equal, if not excel, the imposing example established by God during the Creation. There is no greater paragon for the great and genuine composer, the act of Creation being that for which he most yearns.

Much study in the art of obsession is required. It even might seem that books are blessings, studying truest meditation, but the task that awaits him is incapable of being crushed into academic dust: some such cant, as was the case with his impolitic politics. Music, then, will certainly delight his predisposition for effectual paradox, wake nobility in the soul, and thus remind consciousness of the beauty inherent in things other than the chaotic.

The grand halls of the Vienna opera houses are passages through which many of the finest musical minds have sauntered; indeed, memory alone is all that is required in order to recall their names.

He struggles to represent himself by means which weren't taught to him. The subtle aspects of an act of consciousness remain a child of the night, being so adopted by pale moonlight; he refuses to embrace the luminous rays of an alien sun.

Continuing in this strain of self-discourse, he questions himself: "How is it possible to have universalised such an individualized event? Is my soul sanctioned against expressing the epiphany, or does an arrogant ignorance continue to strike at my efforts with an outstretched arm, a mighty hand?" The questions do not recess, flowing interminably as does a river, with one yet more question flung like dust; only from it to be raised into a fully rekindled flame, continual, rampant:

"Why does it continue to haunt your spirit; what virtue is to be learned from your experience?"

"I find toleration for a question asked out of interest, but yours honours insult and is therefore intolerable."

"I think your previous study," he breaks off into a whisper now; "what was it—Forgetful politics."

"Yes, politics . . . does that not carry more importance than, say, blowing air into a bagpipe?"

"I heard once an alchemist claim that he had invented a certain species of balloon, a most ingenious device he claimed, which itself incapable of exhaustion, is driven to excellence by consuming not only air, being a thing of necessity, but hot air."

"Odd. Are there no preconditions or like penalties to this miraculous mayhem, which this alchemist claims to be a child of ingenuity?"

"Why yes, of course! Do you think the argument airy; by that I mean, my father has chosen this profession, and am I not knowledgeable of pride as a result of his choice."

"Yes, of course I am."

"What, then, but to observe his remark that states that as long as it feeds on the right amounts of exhausted fuels, the invention, which by another name you called mayhem, is all but imperishable, a narrow universality."

"By becoming a composer, and if I am successful being thus, I shall accomplish such signs and wonder as to render any other form of public service, especially the distractive of which you call the bureaucratic, obsolete and grotesque, a monument to princely folly."

"I imagine how I once was unable to imagine the unimaginable. I then seek to secure remuneration."

"When did I first encounter the instruction, the teaching which teaches change to be an indelible part of our world?"

"In the womb, most like."

"What, then? When do I recall hearing what I had experienced first expressed in word?"

"My father. He told me about the bottom of river-beds. Yes, though there is, perhaps, a storm-sick element scarring the surface with turbulence, the deep remains undisturbed by the tempestuous spectacle."

"How did I react to hearing this?"

"Was I apathetic, amazed, alarmed, moved, annoyed; none of what I have thought, all, a few, or these and more?"

"Did this observation inform any of my other decisions?

"Yes, for when I learned of more corpulent bodies of water, having witnessed nature inflicted with greater anger, I then applied my curiosity in accordance to my experience, and questioned my father, asking if what he had said about the river might also be applied to its greater siblings and kindred?"

"Having confirmed my suspicions, I was struck not so much with amazement as with gratitude and obsession."

"Why, then, after observing nature with a discerning intellect, a steady faculty and a healthy curiosity, proceed to entertain the notion of devoting my life to the pursuit of politics?"

"I was obliged to give mercy to my fellow man, to edit the wrongs of His Majesty's sovereignty in order to rise from the ashes of history a phoenix of the hopeful, an agent against which vice and the like evil would have no defence."

"I thought Europe and the whole world a river, didn't I?"

"The object of my studies was to ensure the observation of a natural law?"

"It is, unfortunately, usually astonishing to me how puppeticians, whom habit calls politicians, can render such successful enactments from such appallingly mediocre talent."

"Leaders, then, have learned subtly from the Prince of Ephesus, he who checked once the river of ignorance."

"I wish to repose thither now."

"So many years after the revelation at the river, the Egyptian magic of my chosen subject matter has, at last, been repudiated as an enigmatically appalling hoax.

It nevertheless remains an effectual device, that is, until the time of the Plague of Lice shall return again to the land."

• • • • • •

Full house at the Grand Opera House, not one ticket was left unsold. The seats were gradually being filled, crowds had gathered, with beverages of sobriety and all light refreshments being served, crazed clumsiness in a cocktail being circulated now, fine scents accompanying foul conversations, excruciatingly delicate delights for company with now generously modest colognes, both of which are equally perfuming the air with anticipation and anxiety, recreational gossip, casual occasional exchange, dutiful discussion down in some hallow hallway by the bust of an old moral philosopher, chat, tête-à-tête, banters and natters run rampantly throughout the passageways as guests greeted other guests, acquaintances, colleagues, families, competitors, and neighbours.

Maracelsus has one thought as he sees this now: The audience is impatient, quietly aware of what I am not. Vertiginous composition, he maintained; and so before the performance was to begin, to have been begun, he began thinking about how he had changed behind the curtain, hearing the spectacle which was happening right off stage, that same wretchedness wrenching stage on which he was, then, seeing this.

Music, not merely blood, circulated through his veins; instruments the thoughts of which his intellectual faculty was composed. Hands were more like violin strings than the mere margins of the arm, some minor negligent extension beyond the wrists; eyes, those greatly distant spheres, became the notes of the music for which he fought to perfect during practice session. Patiently attempting to improve some aspect of his art, he brandished humility in the wake of adversity, so beginning the reoccurring cycle of inconstant sense and season, between which he drew no distinction. This he did, but by the promise alone, of music, did he interpret passion's text, the sacred edition in which he found the very same source from which nature had sprung. How shall I gave it to speech, with it being like light from the sun is his relationship to the art, insuperable indivisibility; so, too, was the music within which he conceived himself, soliciting chaos from order.

The dusk with renewed vigour ascends the firmament. The opera house, the harvest of abundant dreams, in the green-evening fields, night's verdurous earth, lies now in like performance to the theatre, in a totality of subtlest abundance.

This is the maestro's last performance.

The audience is seated; quiet but expecting, and the curtains are drawn. The Grand Symphony Orchestra is also seated, unquiet but trusting, like children in the hands of a competent parent, and so the last symphony begins.

The conduction merely continues his mind's conversation with an unseen god; Maracelsus asks himself, "What is this sound that of which I now hear? The orchestra forms what appears to be one great mass or heartbeat, a Panacea of interconnected landmass or facial tissue. The audience is being played upon like some great piano. They who were once masters are now, by reason of the art, purely stripped of either liberty or freedom, and reduced to slaves. Their good music taste binds them to the yoke of the creative, of matter and the touch of distant and mysterious sublimity. They are now part of the performance piece, and so are becoming closer: still more intrigued by what it is that they are hearing now."

The composer is demanding his audience to retrench their realities, if they are to grasp his creativity. What is it to retrench? Their misconceptions of the universe, this business of overspending the currency of prejudice, that is the object with which the composer has concerned himself, its preliminary abridgment. If a flute is introduced to the score, he wishes the audience to decipher its riddle by listening to the music, which is the answer and question conjoined. The union is intimate like the land joined at the hip at present with Poseidon's haughty kingdom, intricate as was Prometheus with intelligent indulgence, it being, then, inevitable as is fate to its fashion.

The composer of "Riparian Emperor" has established now a womb within which the question and answer are one. Scholarly analysis may enhance its enigma, but the composition remains indifferent to the academic spectacle. Maracelsus saw Music once at night, when the mind was deeply buried beneath dream, and it spoke to him, saying, "No other gods shalt thou have before me, for I am a jealous god."

Though Maracelsus is communing with the art, his old classmates, members of the audience, are witnessing the enigmatic violence being perpetrated on the person and soul of that which they are part. The image it conjures up is of an infant ripped from its cradle, and being thrust into the gaping jaws of black revelation, which is receiving by nature, is now truly born.

Maracelsus has forgotten how the audience entered the grand auditorium, ready to be made perishable. His ways may be worded in this way:

"I excused myself from the astonished consciousness of the audience, thus dislodging the item of obsession for which the soldier is honoured. I must choose in contradiction to their calamity; the continual flood in which the world has drowned, and does drown, is not the gravestone upon which I wish to impress the epitaph. I discontinue the black dance of uncertain desires, a silhouette of mist lost amongst velvet vanities.

"To free this feature of fear, to search for an alternative to how I was to be of a piece with myself and make of peace like the wildebeest faced with the dangerous shadows of onslaughts. It is an appetite that I am and one which is to be fed on the past that was in turn starved of the food that is but the dish of dashing presence: its nasty little cookeries. For I had to depart from them, there was no use in using them here, this was a defeat worsened still by a greater difficulty, the source from which I had been assigned geol-cell. I was alone. Like a web weaving together to and from its point any point conceivable to its encompassed extremities, its singing free from either method or technique, it is free and through its resonance it was no less like the wind, as I have so heard it, when it is digested in caves when their bellies are cancerously cavernous-enough.

"The composition is designed to the precision of a dream, enacting on the stage of emotion a drama of universal meaning for the audience."

A harp is played, emphasized, and takes centre stage in the performance now. The tune is light, and becomes only lighter, inviting the listener to go in search of no alternative to how he, the composer, was to map their ways about this mansion, so far away from the mundane, utterly meaningless. And so the audience is lured into serenity, like wildebeest that may be tempted by anxious silence to eat in the green lands. Being watched, not knowing what those who shouldn't have known, do know. But what they probably knew in fear, an "impractical" knowledge.

The piano is struck, striking sure-succession to where the harp left off. The pianist plays that part of the piece most admitting to the foyer of the mansion, the darkness brought by the fallout, of having entered, had yet to obstruct, giving admission to the general beauty of just where the composer is taking them. The large keyboard is only a reflection of its counterpart in the audience's, each emotional key of which operates the godly in the human being, small, feeling, appearance-judging hammer that strikes, only to be struck in return, vibrating an overlapping affection, or web thereof, stretched upon a mental frame, or mind. This too is enclosed, being hidden underneath a hard shell which may assume numerous shapes, various forms. Seven emotions are struck, and their tones range right over to the next, to be led by the violin, no subtle continuation.

Meandering deep around the mansion, the audience feels as if they had spent most of the night thinking or reflecting, as if incessantly shedding the dark to bleed, to yield, to relinquish to them secrets of the moonlight silence. The soft flows of harmonious melodies by the violin string strikes the fluctuations of untouched passion, a flirtation with immortality.

Guitar. The apprehension the audience finds in this stalemate is inconsequential refuse. The sudden sense of hurrying is over; now they are merely being carried.

Maracelsus does not throw thoughts around lightly, and so he sees how they are being returned to a state of nature not too unlike those of degenerate savages. He is sacrificing the name of their illusory pleasures, so that they could allow themselves to satisfy an even more unruly lust than any to be found in those frenzied financial feasts banqueted at world marketplaces. You must know that savages, who are somehow degenerate by whatever means, are such that they are the citizens who do but fancy themselves civilised appendages of the society thitherto concerned. However, they're not only ripe in sophomore angst, but Maracelsus is also young in his unripe solemnity, the desire to redesign in order to return his audience to the original, which is the only design that there is.

The doom of this truth was almost unbearable. Thought, my thought, was then, as it is now and again, and again, and again, all of a sudden interruption, for without the flare of fanfare, may one soon hear occasioned by the music visual vicinity of the prospect.

I am in the audience now, hearing the music of Maracelsus, seeing him drag those who did not wish to let go, and holding hands gently with those few who do not wish to be childish any longer. In little time all were in the art's jurisdiction, being told to be silent and listen.

It was vague, sinister, so much so that when the flute came, it came like a revelation. The chiselling of music began coalescing into an offensive tempestuousness that came to compose my unbridled awareness of what was to come. Clandestine contradiction that it was sure to impress upon consciousness its compositional excellence, a note made harder than the hardness of brute stones, then.

Cello, and with it, Maracelsus writes a poem not with words, but notes, each syllable the presence of realisation.

Their eyes with precious freedom have atoned,
Vowing immortal beauties to secret wit enclose.
If that you have Maracelsus discerned,
Then with apocalypse sweet last concludes.
For once the sharp-toothed enigma being in wound,
To ungrateful ravage the sinister minute
Sings truer virtue and so scorns truthlier quills,
Enacting eternity in presence of the time,
To smear and havoc that which is more than thee.

The music is sombre, alien, and magnificent. The funeral now over, the coffin, into which ignorance has been thrown, is laid as a bed for eternal sleep, an indefinite unconsciousness. A young gentleman looks on, into the distance with which the days provide him, and is finding something in the proud prospect of the future. Old classmates from his student politic days are embarrassed, not believing how much more Maracelsus has become. But they are wrong; he's merely himself. They remember his words,

"Desperation is not to be confused with determination, however. Then again, the distinction is subtle, as there is between justice and revenge. History is as much a product of the imaginative, as it is of the mundane. Truth is not always golden, illusions are oftentimes more dazzling than the sun.

"The desperate heart tends to enslave the imagination so that it is capable of moulding all concepts in its image; its intention is to turn the base metal of an illusion into the pure gold of truth, a matter of fact. Nature. She is recovering from shock, and is preparing herself for sorrow."

The last hand gestures, and the music . . .

Silence.

Scholar by the Warsaw Fire

I hear a mighty music on the wing,
So to silence and stillness shall now I sing?

R. SHLOMOWITZ

It was quiet, and already the lonely streets seemed unburdened by passers-by, and a solitary was pacing in front of flats, between which lies an emptied street, devoid of all human presence but one.

"Nazarich Shlomowitz," the silhouette whispered, disturbing the quietness about him by continuing these repetitions. He persisted in this vein for quite some time, until finally; nature had distracted him, with the harsh hours drawing to a close.

There was a tired calm in the air, feeling much like the one the mind experiences after having been gently woken from a deep sleep.

Nazarich was staring into a puddle now, observing in the reflection the quiet drama, taking place over his head. Slowly, he saw . . . The sun had begun to strike rosy strokes upon the crimsoned rooftops; the darkening horizon was already apparent to the idle and unobservant, and the arrival of pale moonlight had almost seemed swift-footed in its descent on the sleepy village.

"Sir," a voice called out to him.

"Yes," he replied, lifting his gaze from off the puddled floor.

"It's nearly curfew, sir," reiterated the child, before running off, eager to return home again.

Rising to his feet, Nazarich began his way home, only after, when from a discrete distance, he looked back; and saw where he had been sitting, a bench by the gate leading to the old synagogue.

He was accustomed to waiting for the end of the evening service, his intent being to wait for a friend who would pass on his way from the service, and then they would speak to each other, spending the whole evening together. Their discussions provided solace for him, since it was especially refreshing to find a like-minded, intellectually questioning scholar such as himself; quite difficult these days, he thought.

It has been seven months since Nazarich eulogized him, paying for the funeral out of his own pocket-money, and watching on in painful silence as the grave-diggers buried the hollow wooden casket; and hearing the last song sung in order to ensure his soul's salvation.

Excluding the presiding rabbi, the two gravediggers, and six of Nazarich's colleagues from the university, he was the only one truly attending the service: for it was he alone who had known the departed because the young man was an orphan, who never knew his parents. He knew only orphanages when, until he became of the bittersweet sixteenth year, he ran away; abandoning the place that he had been abandoned to . . . wandering the countryside when - almost by accident - he came upon an old synagogue at the centre of the village. Taking shelter by resting himself on a bench, he asked passers-by for nothing, preferring instead to stare into the reflecting waters of a nearby puddle, until an inquiring student, from one of the local yeshivas, saw him, and took the time to speak with him, just to make good conversation, be friendly.

Nazarich, an intelligent, reserved and deeply humane idealistic college student, was moved by what had happened—being haunted himself by memories of an underprivileged and melancholy childhood. The orphan, an inquisitive, imaginative and well-read youth himself, was quick to confide in Nazarich, not concealing in any way the extent to which his fears of the future rose. No matter how much hardened his heart had been, refusing to exhaustively register the appalling excess that his anguish and bewilderment had taken, Nazarich imposed upon himself the singular responsibility of adopting this solitary. Perhaps something hopeful just might come out of it, at least that is how he had argued with himself, not believing how much changed he would become by having accepted to set upon himself this sobering commitment.

The orphanage from which he had escaped was only too pleased to be rid of him, agreeing to the request;

and so Nazarich became his adoptive parent, the sole person to whom the disillusioned adolescent may pledge all his starved affection, and for whom he wished to somehow repay him, for doing what no one else had done, admitting that the word is crippled without the deed; and the deed likewise injured when in absence to the word. For Nazarich was a devout and imposing defender of the doctrines of politic intervention, and being moved, he was by no means shy, let alone timid, when the time was opportune for rampant havoc, and deep-seated, destruction-excessive, cruel chaos-carrying complacency.

He would treat him as if he had been his own brother, blood being inconsequential to the mind and character of his younger sibling, whom he grew to love as much as he had loved once the Master of the Universe himself.

Tonight is an especially painful time for him because when his pocketwatch struck midnight, it marks the anniversary of his brother's death: the seventh year of his successive sorrow, which, no doubt, shall continue to cast its shadow over his mind, whether awake or asleep.

Sick to his stomach with solitude, he decides to visit the cemetery, not caring for curfews or curious currents in the wind, which had appeared almost to be made in the image of the cry, quiet whisperings of confession, inconsolable grief.

The graveyard was devoid of all village presence, but somehow the little lot of ground in which the dead lay buried seemed less emptied than the street, oddly at peace with itself.

Passing the overarching gates, upon which there is impressed various Hebrew inscriptions - he enters, seeing the numerous monuments, headstones, relics and tokens placed throughout its dark grounds; illuminated solely by a pale moon and a few candles of vigil, that yet have to be burned out. Nazarich's slow footsteps trampled over the grass with a burdened mobility, and if seen from a modest distance, his body motion gives the impression of being confined; the weight-imprints he leaves upon the coarse ground reminiscent of prisoners whose legs have been fettered, the natural motion of which appears abused by the soul-corrosive metal, a lingering echo of a tortured constitution.

Perched on a small hill, Nazarich arrived at the point at which he too seemed to have died long ago. The inscription on the monument reads:

Ivan Maximillian Shlomowitz
Beloved Brother of
Rabbi Nazarich M. Shlomowitz

He did not wish to read the entries for his dates of birth and death, preferring to stop in order to prolong a little the approaching surges of grief, which were already beginning to deluge his train of contemplation.

He bends down, and extending his left hand, he touches the cold marble monument: his right knee bent, the slab on which he supports his other hand, he digs his face deeply into his fingers, the wind throwing his hair all about; his battered oldtime trench coat is equally tossed in the air, cool breezes, then cold, its unpredictable movements echoing the suddenness he had felt before entering into combat with it. The officer's coat he had originally worn was noticeably different from what he is wearing now, but once the nation for which he had fought had lost the war, dismissing many of her surviving soldiers into desperation and impoverishment, he decided to fashion out of his sacred Russian garb, a belted raincoat, which reminded him of the carnage that he had been a witness to, when he served in trenches during the Great War.

Coming to this place was never easy, and were it to ever become easy, Nazarich would never forgive himself: for he felt it only natural to be driven to sombre meditation when he came here, anything that fundamentally contradicted this emotion would not only be unnatural for him, but also disgustingly disgraceful against the departed. There are some things that may not be forgotten, especially by emotion, unless we risk inflicting upon the dead a second death: a damnation in which there is hope for salvation. Believing accordingly, seven years made no difference for Nazarich; it might as well have been seven seconds ago: and so were he to live for seventy years, his grief at the loss of his only sibling would be new, each tear: strange, alien, and bitter to him as the opposite emotion is expected from parents who have seen the birth of their first child, proud to see the infant come into the world for the very first time . . . Time is inconsequential, for he has found eternity in the most hatefully nightmarish of places: his grief at the death of his brother. This is hell at its simplest, its most ugly and tormenting form.

Tears had yet to be elicited from him, but sorrow did not need the faulty testimony of such witnesses, for it knew how he was wandering deep inside himself, his whole memory one imposing web of interconnecting fibres of pain, regret, and nostalgia, in which the spider and the fly, its chief object of prey, were fused into a single constitution: Nazarich was made into a witness of the unbearable, a lonely wanderer forced to be turned into a private, inward vision of the truth that most people spend their whole lives running away from. Infinite loneliness: cosmological holocaust.

"What greater menace than that, so much orderly madness . . ." he says, whispering into the wind.

The silence was then suddenly disturbed . . . Nazarich saw two soldiers in the distance, their torches giving a clear indication that one was drunk, the other observant somehow, as if he was deliberately looking for some Jew who had broken curfew.

Nazarich was steadfast; he wasn't about to be encroached by two vulgar intruders, that same uniquely despicable species of scum that had taken everything away from him. Nazarich was tired, and so he sat down, trying to remember better days which never were, except in the imagination.

A shout, "Go there, Boris! For I'll inspect the graveyard: you, the temple."

Nazarich continued to remain where he was, until, eventually, he was interrupted by a harsh voice, calling out to him. The soldier who had been particularly watchful was now standing beside him, a torch in his hand, with both of their faces revealed solely by means of that single flame.

"Jew," he shouted, "is it not curfew, already?"

"Russian, ever since I lost my brother, I have been living under a permanent and more pressing curfew; it is my life; and with my loss, all other like prohibitions are either illusory or insignificant: usually both, like yours," his reply was soft-spoken, but panged, as if every word that he had uttered was tied down by some unseen shackle, preventing a certain natural freedom in speech to proceed unhindered by any want or need to communicate. The voice gave the impression of a child's, who did not want to be parted from its mother. A desire for silence, then, was what he had wanted; his speech wasn't a tool of communication in his hands, but rather a device of distraction that just might lead into destruction. The soldier thought his tone of voice haunting, a ghost seen in distant fields, casually wandering an abandoned countryside; but in seeing it the world in which you thought you lived was turned upside down, a calamitous transformation.

"Get up, Jew. Now!" The sheer malice in the reply was indubitable, and now, so it would seem to Shlomowitz, the outcome inevitable.

Nazarich rose in his own time, after which he continued to remain silent.

Turning his gaze, inspecting the area in order to be certain of their privacy, the soldier leaned forward into Nazarich's right ear, as if to whisper.

"Sir," he said now with his voice riddled in as much politeness as there is pressingness; "please listen to what I have to tell you. Eighteen days from now, on your holiday Passover, there's going to be a liquidation of the ghetto. The Tsar intends to confiscate all your lands, taking everything away from you in order to redistribute it to wealthy landowners and industrialists, so that he might turn a profit, being that the economy is bankrupt."

Nazarich interjected, saying, "There're over thirty-five thousand of us, here in the ghetto: pregnant women, underfed children, cripples, retired communities, whole families, injured and impoverished; generations, then, young and old; how does the Tsar intend to relocate us? He's taken our village; now you tell me he has his eyes set on the ghetto. Is the intention royal to have us forfeit our lives?"

The soldier placed his hand on Nazarich's left shoulder, squeezing tightly, saying, "You'll be given six days to evacuate the ghetto. Any who fail to do this will be shot, on orders from the General."

"What is this; we are seventy miles away from any town or village: we have no means of transporting ourselves anywhere during that meagre amount of time. Look around you, such a journey would mean certain calamity for over half the Jewish population!"

"There's more to fear than that, rabbi. If after eighteen days you have been found homeless, without refuge or support from foreign powers, we have been given orders to trace your footsteps, to hunt you down, and when you and your people have been found, we are to begin—" he paused, as if for fear . . . of losing his position while wandering in mist, dazed and confused; "begin shooting you indiscriminately. We have not been given orders to take any prisoners. Don't inflict, I beg you, a panic upon the village, for then none will survive. The world must know what is about to happen . . . pray to your God, rabbi. Warn your people now, prepare them: save only those you can."

Finishing his confession, the young soldier stepped back, giving a tortured gaze at Nazarich, as if to ask for forgiveness; knowing that what he had done was unpardonable. The soldier took his leave of him, vanishing into the quiet of the night.

There's no irony in emotion—Nazarich wasn't so much in disbelief, as he was in disgust. The architects of the ghetto weren't apparently pleased with what they had done, executing this latest invention would be in keeping with an imperial agenda that didn't seek intermediate sufferance, but indeed, called for a removal indefinite from Russian society: a solution to be achieved in the liquidation of the ghetto. The purpose for which they had been chosen to be relocated here was now known to him, their forced resettlement was the gradual means by which the ambition for annihilation would begin to have engineering, and soon executing, their collective death, a "perpetual extinction" being the aim in definition to all their actions. But it was one thought that haunted most his mind: *Save those you can, all the rest shall die.*

Nazarich left the graveyard, returning to the village, which itself will soon become its grandiose addition.

The streets were now entirely deserted, all the lights in homes had been extinguished; and only a few torches and lanterns hung from designated walls in order to make those who had broken the curfew easy targets for swift reprisal from patrolling soldiers, and a few more drunken, mercenary night watchmen.

It's strange, still, to see the alleyways, were softly illuminated by torchlight; their features were indiscriminate in the flickering moonlight, whereas their original colours stubbornly maintained the austere impressions of pale blue, grey, and various dyes of brown, all of which would have been quite apparent during the labouring hours for the imprisoned.

Making his way quietly from the narrow street corners, the tired scholar arrived home, or what was now his provisional residence. It was a simple eight-story apartment complex, dark and derelict. The foyer was covered with hay, and the stairway leading up to his flat was brittle; the creaking reverberations of footsteps always echoed throughout the building, no matter if it was day or night. The echo of each step he took ricocheted, further impressing upon his already troubled consciousness, a sense of approaching menace that would soon take away what little had been left for his people. Death–so he should contend–was to be their last inheritance, a final registry cataloguing a history devoid of either vindication or redemption, but becoming instead, a sinister testament to the malicious meticulousness with which their tormentors pursued their destruction: a monument to God's disturbing mysteries.

The door unlocked, swung opened, Nazarich threw himself on the sofa, thinking nothing but feeling everything. "Hope is usually wrinkled skin on the face of fear", is an old saying which is never in disagreement to the rabbi's unique frame of mind, but refusing to indulge himself in motionless contemplations, he arose from off the sofa in a manner that was unnatural to his accustomed habit. This habit is defined by his committing to analysis the situation, plotting the actions with which he would later decorate the face of activity: with a meticulous predisposition for divining uncertainty which would have befitted a seasoned general; especially when many battles have been lost, and there is one left that might tip the scale in his favour. It was in this manner that he did now commit to studying the way in which he carried himself during the day; and again, later in the night. But not now . . . He shut the door, gently, and began pacing again, an activity that became his sole means of claiming himself a participant in the act of physical exercise.

The following morning, he heard the banging on the door.

"Rabbi, Rabbi!" a voice called out to him.

Nazarich had fallen asleep atop his study table, and being thus awakened, walked unhurriedly to the door, his feet dragging across the wooden floor.

"Good morning, Yakov," he said, as he opened the door.

"Oh, come, Rabbi! Olga's been blessed with child!"

Before Nazarich could wrench a reply from himself, Yakov took his hand and hurried him down the hall, where his room was situated.

Upon entering, the tired scholar saw Olga, Yakov's reserved spouse, holding her child in loincloth, the observances properly committed considering what little the ghetto had.

"*Mazel tov*, Olga," he said softly, though the inclination was to have had uttered *mazel tov* not as a celebratory salutation. The young rabbi's salutation was not for the purpose of wishing them well with the child, but to wish them well with their and their child's survival. The celebratory, congratulatory acknowledgement had been converted into the subtlest welcoming for woe in wretchedness yet uttered. Nazarich, though, thought it enough to have the Master of the Universe see to such things.

"Thank you, Rabbi. Oh please, come see him," she said, her exhausted tone secured in its serenity.

"He has your hands," he commented.

"Would you like to hold him?"

"No . . .—I'm clumsy."

She began gesturing, "Please, Rabbi."

Nazarich, being taken by temperance, took the fragile infant, and held him close. He looked intently into his quiet face, calmly wrapped in sleep. Yakov and Olga looked intently at him, too, to see if they could detect any discernable emotion from his face other than pain and exhaustion. Nazarich seemed distant and warmly expressionless, until, finally, his mind returned to the soldier's revelation from yesternight, an anxious appearance rippling through his face: the ghetto will be liquidated.

"Olga, you are right to have thanked the Master of the Universe for this blessing," he said, returning the child to her; "I pray that he may continue to secure the blessing which he has bestowed upon you and your family.

"Now I must leave. Please carry my warmest regards to both your families."

"Yes, of course, Rabbi," Yakov replied.

Nazarich gestured by arching himself a little; then proceeded to walk out the door. The weight of the terrible secret he carried within himself weighed him down, like heavy boulders atop his burdened shoulders.

"God, the Holy One, has blessed them and now he has burdened me in informing them of the curse that he has prepared for them," he asides.

He returns to his flat. The creaking footsteps emitting from the wooden floorboards, hollow and splintered, are quickly followed by their ricocheting from off the building's damaged high-rising walls. It's a reoccurring example of how uncertainty–once distant and mysterious, a Morpheus-like hypothesis to be espoused by the disciple-dreamer alone almost–is the only certainty now for the faithful, overworked, hungry inhabitants of the ghetto. Shutting the door gently, resuming his pacing, he sits himself down; and burying his face deep into his hands, as if he were some actor ready to go off stage in order to refresh his senses for the next performance, he raises his face to stare at the window, and be reminded of the world outside, a stage from which he may not exit at any time until the last act has come.

He sees that there's a transparent reflection of his person projecting from its dirtied surface. His shadow, being enlarged by the angular cornered holes in the roof through which some additional light creeps—keeps creeping in, forms a third representation of his troubled nature: a twilight witness to his awful duty.

The title, "Rabbi", was a reminder of a previous existence for Nazarich, whose family had been orthodox Sephardic Jews, adamant defenders of the faith, even when all appearance betrayed the fact that the faith wasn't adamantly defending them during their numerous, almost unendurable tribulations.

Yeshiva was unavoidable, and nor was it to be avoided. He was eager to begin his rabbinical studies, being fully conscious of the responsibilities not only to himself but also to his people, when, expectantly, he accepted the solemn duty of becoming a virtuous custodian of the sacred tradition; that would always weigh upon him.

Youth was that time when hope was a constant mistress, indulging benevolent irrationality with sometimes necessary lies with which to persuade a searching intellectual, not pleased by either dogma or blind orthodoxy. He didn't mind fervent worship or fierce worshippers, far from it. For, indeed, he welcomed such emotional testimonies in the synagogue: finding them healthy and healing. It was when orthodoxy overrode compassion in the face of contemplating the possible but menacing, when defending God became synonymous with an unspoken concurrence to attack the victim, should either his sufferance or philosophy be a contradiction in living terms of the sacred words; this he found idolatrous, appalling, and the most ingenious and fundamental invalidation to the faith of his fathers. It was intolerable.

He left the temple and began teaching at a university. Being relocated to the ghetto was an injury too deep to overlook or argue away, and so whenever, after having adopted Ivan, his young brother wished to attend the service, he would wait for him outside, on a bench, until they were ready to go to the streets, debating and being quiet together.

He was twenty-eight when he had adopted Ivan, and lost him not a year later when he was shot dead by a soldier for "breaking curfew". Ivan heard a child crying outside, and leaving the safety of the apartment, entered the streets and grabbed the child to pull him to safety. Nazarich was a deep sleeper, who was also hard of hearing, but had been woken by an uneasy dream he had had that night. He heard lamentations originating from the streets, a child's voice. He knew what had happened, and shutting out, he rushed down the stairs, nearly falling upon himself, until he saw Ivan; by the time he got halfway inside, the bullet had been permanently lodged in his cranium, killing him instantly.

The child was frozen, and didn't hint at motion. Nazarich shut the door, and held Ivan: he had grown cold. His brother's blood spilled quickly on top of the floor, Nazarich's hands and arms, until he appeared the infant of a giantess who had been taken out of the womb. Nazarich's tears fell as fast as Ivan's blood had gushed; and the whole building had been woken, its residents haunted by the memory to this day.

The child was Yakov's firstborn son, Herkom-Yitzhak, whom was usually referred by his name's latter, more easily recognisable portion. Yakov and his wife, Olga, had been spending the night with family, celebrating the birth of one of his sister's children, when young Yitzhak decided to wander off; the child too curious by standards established by his own alone, no one saw him leave until it was too late. By the time Yakov returned home, no more than thirty minutes after his son had taken off alone, he saw Ivan dead in the hands of a knee-bent Nazarich, covered in his blood, with Yitzhak dying of fever not two months later, the physician suspecting pneumonia.

Since then, Nazarich has found the sight of blood intolerable, a hateful token that terror had brought him. For Yakov and Olga, having lost their only child, they started all over again. They had secretly agreed to invite Nazarich to the birth only when much of the blood had been cleaned and removed, in order to honour Nazarich's expressed wish not to see blood unless absolutely unavoidable.

Thirty-three now, Nazarich understood himself anciently: a distant relic of some mysterious past that would never be able to return again. His childhood had been transparent glass through which he saw a bleak and muddy future, yet he saw some flicker of hope creeping in through the ubiquitous bandages of his solitary consciousness, which had not really hoped for redemption. It came, only to be taken away from him at the end. His adolescence and early adulthood were once unwrapped presents of possibility, so much for them! And for the future, it was overshadowed by the menace of Imperial Russia's heart-hardened Tsar.

Nazarich slid opened the window, leaning slightly in order to see the passers-by down there making their rounds of daily grind. Their dizzying repetitions had begun to remind him of a conversation he had had with Professor Victor Slavensky, a colleague from the university:

Looking out the window, with his gaze distorted by unuttered emotions, he began speaking barely above a whisper, "We have lived in the ghetto for the past seven years, in constant fear and continual impoverishment, without so much as our voice ever being heard from beyond the rooftops."

Fidgeting with his hands as he did with what he had said; his colleague threw his thoughts into the air, "When did the world ever worry itself about the welfare of the Jews, Nazarich?"

"Victor, it's usually either when we're working, thus stimulating a bankrupt economy; or when we're dying, and in so doing contributing to industries which profit handsomely from our deaths. This, also, stimulates the morally bankrupt minds of its architects. For in these ways, has the world really and truly ever cared about our people, Victor."

"And what do you want me to do about it, change it?" he said, suppressing the desire to shrug his shoulders.

Temporarily turning his eyes towards him, he addressed him directly now, "Not that I wouldn't mind, but since you're speaking realistically and not hypothetically, all I would like you to do about this is simply acknowledge that the situation in the ghetto is quite hopeless; and as for God, go tell him, when you pray to him, that if he's trying to tell us something, he's doing well in reminding our sceptical impulses that there just might be nothing special about either our world, let alone ourselves. Do, too, at least on my behalf, congratulate him on having the largest congregation, it being not a community but slaves, nations, paupers, kings, these whole too-much hot, cold-hearted heavens, while being the poorest communicator I yet have ever known. You would think a congregant would have tired of tawdry diatribe, call it our sufferance, and threatened taking the bemah over for himself by now."

"I can't, Nazarich."

"And why is that, Victor?" he interjected, and studying the silence which had befell the room, he asked him now, "Why do you find my first proposition so spiritually unbearable, if not wholly abhorrent? Shall I take a tongue and give it word with which to speak?"

Resigning himself to the doorpost, leaning against it, he sighed, "You're going to have to."

Nazarich looked at him as he spoke, "All right, then. If you were to submit to my request, and admit that the situation here is just that, quite hopeless, you'll be officially stripping hope from off your battered carcass of desire, feeding fear; without which not only would you be deprived of justifiable ignorance, but also, and this is the real tenth plague for you, you'll be effacing the very means by which faith is founded. Namely, the orphan's secret way of imagining he'll see his lost father again. Take hope away, and you'll be left with a truly devastating decision to make, either you renounce your fairytale notions, or you'll announce deep inside yourself, Victor, that complacency and ignorance are not the way in which to go about solving the problems of your discomfort with the world, escaping the otherwise conscious desire to touch the problems directly."

"What do you want, Nazarich: money, fame, a better social station, finer foods, a bigger study room . . . aren't you ever satisfied with what God has given you? Isn't there just as much to be thankful for, if not more so?" he asked, throwing his hands into the air.

"What has he given me, Victor? Since your memory is shorter than I had initially thought, I shall have to rekindle the spark." And moving authoritatively, his thoughts aptly expressed with a wave of the hand, he resumed:

"I was given life when death had taken my sister. God took my mother away from me when our village was destroyed. I held her as she lay dying; my whole body was bathed in her blood. My father's now a cripple who can't tell the difference between night and day, not that there is much, if any, difference between the two, nowadays. Before reaching maturity, you and I and our whole village was crushed into this god-forsaken, isolated, impoverished, disease-carrying, good-for-nothing hole. Now we can't dance or even sing our praises to the Master of the Universe for giving us *so much*, such an extravagant opportunity to suffer! It's as if every living, breathing moment throws the door of experience open to fresher torture chambers, the latest horrors with which to torment the mind to madness! I do not wish to be granted artificial compensations for being cursed with divine annihilations, like Job. I mean, my dear Victor, if we have to suffer, so as to sing God's praises, then our contribution will erect a hymn, which if made into a physical structure, shall be closer to heaven than the tip of the Tower, whose true-fixed and godlike state did cause envious portents in the heaven."

Nazarich had returned to his sitting position by the window, a breeze striking the face, and yet his words remained as tortured as ever, hopeless utterances, "Shall I tell all those who mourn that they may not question God, and with a thoughtless speech, tell them to be silent, have their mouths shut-up, the awful silence, then, fire for our faith?

"If a father has lost a son, shall I slay the soul: doing to it what has been done to the body of his child?

"If a son has lost a father, am I to begin doing God's good work again; inflicting upon his anguished mind a second violence, which would be no less terrible than the first? Shall I defend God's honour by these time-honoured means? Committing in this way not deicide but spiritual homicide, which I call *spiricide*; is the price of self-sustained peace in the spiritual sphere to be secured only with the blood of those who have bled, at the cost of attacking the victim, again? Truth—"

Knocking on the door, Nazarich's stream of thoughts is interrupted.

Opening the door, Nazarich is quick to greet his guest, "Ah, Victor; I was just thinking about you. Please come in."

"Thank you, Nazarich," he replies.

"Tell me, Victor, what has brought you to me at this god-forsaken hour; I know you're one not to be up before afternoon."

"I need to ask you a question, Nazarich."

"I'm listening."

"I don't know how to express what I know in simpler terms, unless I risk inviting digression into the fray," he paused, attempting to suppress an anxious reticence in his voice; "there's talk—there's going to be an uprising."

"When . . . ?" he asked. .

"Soon . . . probably . . . it'll be before Passover."

Nazarich knew that any hint of insurgence would spell certain death for them; the soldier had warned of a plot calling for their destruction. What a perfect opportunity to do this injustice with impunity under the guise of self-defence!

"I wrote these lines quite some time ago; I would like you to read them to yourself."

"Nazarich, are you serious? I mean, now—"

"Yes, now," he interjected.

"Very well, then. Let me see."

Nazarich handed him a sheet of paper with these words impressed upon it:

How shall we say a syllable written first in tears?
To write of death's havoc unto the touch
Of innocence, yet not scarred by nature's
Withering vines or slithering untimely lines,
Is but to pronounce unto thee sacred solemnity's
Troth; and yet how now the memories lied?
Once with loss and fears thou hast in sooth died.

Echoes in the memory 'tis,
Passion pronouncing,
Yet how doth thee and thy heart miss
Fashions once announcing.

Is the memory but the monument?
The times, O! the times! What times is time?
Serpentine sorrow hath slithered into mine heart,
Cracking vindictive vein in the valour's arm,
Tossing the vessels in mine head as like sea
Unto the thrust unsuspecting sailor.
If this be but purpose, blind am I to its design:
But despair shall I not, for death that comes to thee
Shall with a gentle blow come at last to me?

For in death shall greater purpose be known,
But must I die to detail what thou, my Lord, hast sown?
What in reason shall ruin the purpose thus
That I must be in sooth rendered first to dust?

Symphonic strength, echoing joy!
I am by the truth's vocation alone.

To walk on the piercing ice of sorrow,
With robe but barely clothed, naked at the feet,
And at a pace so in sooth slow upon
That the horrid distance for fear of the fall
Is to truly tread on terrain when angels
At heart fear to traverse,
Thus 'tis as like to write the verse.

Antique citadel, beloved nation mine!
War hath the wound bleeding seen, moments
Decaying, histories by hatred forged thus.

I hear a mighty music on the wing,
So to silence and stillness shall now I sing?

"Nazarich, I don't—"

Sighing, he said, "They're going to resettle us on this coming Passover holiday."

"What! Where?" he exclaimed, more than asking.

"We must manage that for ourselves; we have not a month in which to prepare, no assistance shall be given."

"I mean, there's no . . . we'll die, Nazarich!"

"That's their objective. Come, we must tell the others now, before God chooses otherwise . . .

Rhetoric of the Demonic

Heschel: When things are not right, Akeiden is genius orphaned to chaos?

Akeiden: There is hope.

Heschel: And if the situation is quite hopeless?

Akeiden: Then it's not wise to accept things as they are, being that they are not right.

Heschel: Why is that?

Akeiden: The attempt would be to adapt to what is wrong, accepting the decision to have abandoned what is right.

Heschel: If this is done now there would be nothing at all that is right.

Akeiden: It is, then, when genius is orphaned by chaos; being only later adopted by madness.

I remember faithfully enjoying my usual habit of throwing stones into the school pond, watching the concentric circles ripple across the surface. This simple pastime reminded me of how this modest beginning, a pebble tossed, may lead on account of uncertainty to such astonishing endings.

The gymnasium I attended–which by its modern name is called secondary school–was mediocre to its essence, squeezing the commonplace at its simplest to its most wretched compression.

My parents, but my peers especially from earlier school years, had frequently informed me about the vicious contradictions, and virtuous intentions which I would encounter upon my entering the gymnasium, which was by this time infamous in the registry of my social perception; if for no other reason that I had heard too many miserable stories about it. I was told, and in some rather subtle language, how I would come to grasp the appallingly intricate masterpiece of this social monstrosity; call it high school, the prime primitive paradox by which we have chosen to understand nightmares, reason s solitary dream chamber, at least thus far.

I began where I did not wish to begin. But . . . that's how I understood the ending, not wishing to begin again at the beginning, but having to. What is worse about being right is when nobody listens, for those who listen do not understand, and as for those who did not, or could not, they remain children even when there's nothing left but a shrivelled body whose mind, its prime instrument, is then haunted by memories: the ghosts of the past. I do not wish to either accept or adapt to ignorance, preferring no substitute for scathing truth.

I was certain of this; especially when my father, a hard-drinking Catholic, had lost his job at the bank; and having deprived us of either hope or history, his attitude towards the family was generous to the point at which

I drew the limit of savagery which I have observed in nature, the wild specimens thereof.

I had begun by being publicly schooled, but this didn't work, and so I continued in this fashion until my father lost his first job, during which he engaged in certain illegal activities, the specificity of which I need not recount as it is of no consequence to the reader, in order to ensure financial prosperity for his family. All the same, what I'll say is that bribery and embezzlement were the chief blemishes on his professional resume.

My father had, fortunately, secured much wealth before his tenure at the bank; and so when we moved, after he had found employment there, this "morally orthodox" transformation introduced me to my first private school, where I learned how to be taught by my instructors, finding the practice eccentric but rather enjoyable, I must say. It is truly to my profound surprise that in public schools, as is confirmed by the majority memory, the student is accustomed to being taught by his or her self, so as to find any other learning style odd, if not obscenely unorthodox, to say so little of the matter. Upon entering an "elite" education, I was taken aback by being taught how I was to be taught by my teachers, rather than the student teaching himself. An ingenious proposition, isn't it?

Following the fall of my father, the family went almost bankrupt, and I was taken out of what had been my accustomed manner of living. So I began public school afresh my memories of my private schooling.

Yes, my fond reflections of public education strike me like a sledgehammer to the jawbone; it is unsuspecting as it is sudden. I am accustomed to underpaid teachers who claim ignorance as the mask behind which they hide the face of truth, yet earnestly protesting the profound disease that has courted public education with indifference, refusing to acknowledge how this courtship begets both apathy and annihilation. These incompetent bureaucrats are capable concubines, which belonging to princely dangers, have grown accustomed to being casually loved by the gentle manners of a seaman who has not known affection for far too long. The greatest textbook I have thus far read in a public school is Folly's, since she is the headmistress over whom distraction and destruction alone have priority. Public school is, then, what happens when the wolves have persuaded the sheep to come out to play, in order to better acquaint themselves—I think the marriage of madness is next to follow when dinner is ready to be served, for a hungry society starves of manners in the face of unruly sense, no matter how uncommon.

So much has changed now . . .

I woke when I heard the school bus leaving; I saw from my window the means by which I was to enter and exit school, to impatiently vanish into the distance. My mother was not pleased, but I managed to persuade her that the walk from home to school was not particularly remarkable. She was persuaded, but not that I had much art in my arguments because even if she weren't late for work herself, she would have been unable to drive me to school anyway. Had she arrived to work–a full forty-five minute drive–any more late, I suspect she would have been laid off, and indefinitely.

The shower over, my person fully dressed and adorned with the necessary baggage, I impressed my kiss upon my mother's cheek, and left for my first day of school. This gave me an inviting opportunity to contemplate certain matters without which I wouldn't have been able to find myself here, in a new and distant place. My father had taken his own life, but only after he'd thought he had done the same with the woman in whom he claimed to have glimpsed the face of God himself. My mother refused to indulge the mind with detail that she considered superfluous, and so I remained unaware of the particulars of her miraculous survival for quite some time.

We came to an unfamiliar place in order to escape a place that had become unfamiliar, and so the intention was to re-enact that old phoenix drama without which fairy stories could not be made possible. I was a very lonely individual at this stage of my life; I remain to this day.

Yes, I remember now. I walked to school that first day, passing the tranquil nests of homes on my way. I distinctly recall my first impression of seeing the front edifice of the building, which, though still slightly hid by distance, was becoming clearer as I approached the signs welcoming the student to the "Home of the Phoenixes". The school's official mascot is the lion; this was made the more curious when I later found out that the official slogan of the school had once been "Home of the Lions" which would explain why two lions had graced the entrance.

I went to the cafeteria, in the hopes of striking a conversation with someone. See if I would be welcomed on my first day. I walked in, I saw a girl reading a book; and since she was the only student doing so, I wished to strike a conversation with her who–perhaps–might be of a like disposition towards good books.

Coming to a stop at the front of the table, I asked her permission to sit down next to her. She gave me permission by gently waving her head, as her word complemented her utterance in the affirmative: "It's a free country."

She had yet to look at me; but once a few other students had done so, I was approached. The two students who approached me *introduced* themselves as Nick and Josh; they stood to my right, the girl sitting opposite.

"Are you Jewish?" asked Josh. I suspect that their seeing my Star of David neckpiece had prompted the question.

"I am, yes." Having replied in this way, I sensed the girl next to me readying for some discomfort; she seemed to be fidgeting somewhat.

"It's a Jew! Well, Nick, I'd never . . ." Josh exclaimed.

"Don't call him that."

"Why not, Nick?" *I wonder if they realised I was right in front of them, hearing this.*

"He *shan't* answer my question, unless you call him by his name."

"Whatever makes you happy!" he paused, in order to suppress further laughter; "So, what's your name?" his tone mocking now.

"My name's Akeiden "

"What?" they both blurted, interrupting me.

"My name is Akeiden, Akeiden "

"Weird Jew names," his tone became deriding, and continuing in this vein; "why can't you have some normal name?"

I interjected. "You mean, a popular Christian name."

Josh looked pleased, as if his ignorance had been vindicated. He said, "Right, like Jacob or Michael; mine, especially."

"And what is your birth name?" I asked.

"It's Joshua."

I was dealing with the ignorant.

"Do it sanely," Nick whispered to his friend.

"Akeiden?"

"Yes, Joshua."

"My friend needs— "

"I would like to ask you a question!" Nick exclaimed, his interruption laboured.

"I'm listening."

"Why did the Jews use crucifixion as their form of capital punishment?"

"The ancient Jews didn't use crucifixion either as a form of punishment or admonition."

"Then what was it?"

"For a large class of cases, Nick, it was stoning."

"Why didn't you stone Jesus, then?"

"You would have to go ask an Italian."

"Why?" he asked; his tone puzzled, but sceptical.

"We didn't crucify him, the Romans did," I was becoming aggravated now.

"I thought you said we should go ask an Italian?" Nick's companion asked.

"Josh, was Jesus Jewish?"

To which he replied, "No, of course not." His demeanour had become unusually relaxed, hinting at his sense of conviction in the answer he had given me.

"What was he then?"

"That's a silly question, Akeiden; seeing how you're the one with the glasses. He was Christian." His cocksureness had multiplied, giving no sign of doubt or disbelief.

"I see; and who told you this?"

"My dad."

"Has your father ever taken drugs?"

"He has," he answered sincerely.

"Then that explains it."

"How?"

"He was stoned when he told you this," I did not wish to continue this charade, so I allowed honesty to take hold of my tongue; "Bloody blockheads! Why do you continue in crucifying my good opinion of you hapless goys? I mean, do you take some kind of profound pleasure in crucifying us; we who are the direct descendents of the man whom you call—"

Having said this, the girl sitting next to me interjected, asking me a question: "Why did you want to sit next to me?"

Nick and Josh were listening intently now.

I replied in earnest, "To talk to you, to see what you were reading."

"Let's get something straight, Jew," here it comes, I thought; "You're not going to get your Jew Christ-killing nail into my Christian cross, so just—!"

"I just wanted to talk," I said, my tone puzzled.

She wasn't going to have intercourse with reason, so she continued, "You're not going to be plucking this flower, buddy! I know your kind, dirty Jew shmuck; this is sexual harassment."

"What, I—?"

She arose irascibly from the table, continuing her diatribe, " . . . Jews—"

Once she had left, Nick and Josh also took their leave of me; their laughter an echoing ridicule . . . I couldn't bring myself to believe what had happened, but, fortunately, the scene had been self-contained. The episode was restricted to Nick, Josh, the girl who accused me of sexual advances, and myself.

I decided to avoid any further trouble; I wished to visit the school library. Arriving there, I was greeted by a sign that informed me about the library being closed for the first fortnight of school.

Not believing my run of bad luck, I tried to secure a glimpse of the inside by looking through the window adjoining the left door, setting my backpack down on the ground. As I peered in, taking my time, I saw a decent collection of books, but not wanting to further indulge my discontent by staring at what I could not have: I decided to take out a book and just begin reading by the entrance. Searching my backpack over, I couldn't find the book until I saw a small note, a torn piece of notebook paper, saying, "Book got bored."

What is—I looked in both directions, and to my immediate right, I saw a student with a book like mine running off into the distance. He'd just about vanished by the time I saw him, though I was able to capture an idea of the kind of clothing he had on.

The bell rang, exasperating whatever calm sense I might have had earlier, and not wishing to suffer any further surprises, I showed myself to class. Walking burdenly, random concerns began occupying me. I thought about my father, who was a non-believing Catholic; and how he ever managed to understand my mother, a non-believing Jew.

My thoughts could not crystallize themselves into concrete contemplation, owing to the languorous havoc coursing through the hallways. Entering thus, the students were dizzying in their meandering motions, to-ing and fro-ing like some kind of lost child in an orphanage, or, perhaps, a mouse being chased by some corpulent cat.

I found my class not too far off from the mark of tardiness, the bell belching as I came in. I wanted to repose somewhere. So when I found a vacant desk at the corner of the classroom overlooking the school grounds, I sat down; and not wanting to waste anymore time, I took some reading material out of my backpack.

I began reading an old letter I had written to a publisher:

To Sir,

My name is Akeiden Campos. I am a seventeen-year-old student from the Homeland. Needless to say, you do not know who I am, nor have we ever met. But I have talked to you, briefly, over the telephone in regards to this letter.

To begin with, my contacting you is an act of importance. Let there be no doubt whatsoever about that. I composed this letter because I need assistance, and here I have explained myself in no uncertain terms. I ask that you please exercise patience with the way in which I have written this note.

When I was fifteen, I wrote a tome. At the time of its completion, all I was doing was exercising my abilities; but . . . now I don't think this. It was a gift from G-d, but like anything else given from the Giver, Who is also a recipient, the gift is as much a blessing, as it is also a curse.

What I wrote is a Jewish digest. I know that what I have written has the potential of getting my family out of the dark chasm, into which we have been thrown. This is why I have contacted you.

My father has lost his job; he has lost five jobs in the course of seven years, and he doesn't fail in continuing to do this. In fact, it's the only thing he's really good at: losing things. Now with my father unemployed, my mother works. She makes a minimum wage salary, which barely pays the bills. My grandmother is sick, and is going to have an expensive surgery; she is unable to help us. All the families through my mother's side are destitute, aide cannot be asked of them; indeed, we used to provide for them. The family through my father's side has declined, citing old feuds to excuse their behaviour.

All the money that was saved to pay for my college tuition is gone; used to buy food. This continues to this day, and I live the present with the means by which I sought to secure my future. I was in England, actually, at the gymnasium, when this hell became part of our daily activities. I was deregistered last year, because I was unable to pay the fees. My family has many debts to pay off, more than you can possibly imagine; and as for a loan my father has tried, but the responses he has received were outright rejections, the same with my mother.

I'm going to stop here because the list just goes on and on; and I don't wish to complain, but putting into words my disposition feels distasteful and pointless. It is useless to protest about these things, but too many times has life struck me like sculpture, my dear sir, because it is cold in nature, some form of life made from lifeless substance, a magnificent artifice . . . but if–as so was the case with Pygmalion–we find ourselves staring at our work, and it is in turn staring at us, speaking to us, more alive–perhaps–than we, who are its creators, then we are vindicated: more appreciative of the Creation than any of the other created.

Due to my determination to do something for my family, I went back to my work. It lay scattered all throughout my room, at the time. I have sent manuscripts to publishers everywhere, but all I got back were rejection letters: an index of euphemisms, so much excellent rubbish.

As was the case with the ancients, I believe that writing is a gift given to the writer directly from G-d. In the days immediately preceding my birth, I was found worthy of receiving the treasured gift. His Servants have found me lacking in credentials, which is to say, I have been found either inept or expendable.

You may think, however, that I am deluding myself. The publishers are qualified professionals; and am I not an upstart, a kingdom of obscurity: my name no more recognizable than the identity of the Pyramid builders? This line of argument would have Truth say that my narrative mustn't be any good, but as you are probably aware of, there're many celebrated authors going back to the last century, whom Time chose to deny publication, then recognition. This is done repeatedly, so as to spin the wheel full circle.

I wanted to have my book self-published, as these authors had done, but I am unable to provide the necessary resources. I am for want of the material means. I've sought employment, but I came up empty, always.

I need to speak to someone who can help me, who shan't outright dismiss me; like the way in which Pharaoh had dismissed Moshe.

If an individual of culture and patience could see what it is that I have written, read a page with print which I have impressed upon it, they would see for themselves why my book asks to be read. My work concentrates on the Diaspora by having the Jewish experience crystallized in words, but in words and ways that no contemporary book has managed to achieve, which is to say, that like Moses who had to begin at the beginning and teach the Hebrews beginnings, I too have begun at the beginning and I am ready to teach these beginnings.

My claim, in of itself, may appear arrogant, but Joseph had a cloak of many colours; and so does truth.

To say that I am poorly resourced would be a lie, because my family's financial disposition is desperate. Judaism means to wrestle with G-d; and through my wrestling, I am seeking to inspire a Jewish cultural reawakening. My work is different because the book was born from spiritual reticence, but necessitated by material want. Creativity above all, however, gave me continuity.

People say to me that they sympathize with my situation. However, they say also that they are afraid that they cannot be of any help. But my call for help is not just about publishing novels, but about establishing and enhancing the Jewish literary scene, a defining feature of a healthy future for its people.

I have continued to try to contact publishers directly, but I have been turned away. Literary agents have as much obedience as did Lucifer. I am not exaggerating; experience is my teacher, and it is the most brutal form of instruction. I know that it's not easy to get things published, but I am patient and persistent. In the meanwhile, however, it is probably wise to seek another source of income, but I have tried, and failed. Fate is my hardened heart, as far as I am concerned. Very few writers, in truth, can actually make enough money through their writings to support themselves. Most have other jobs: many are teachers, some drive taxis; in short, they hold many varied kinds of jobs. I am like Job, then: jobless.

Regarding my family's financial difficulties, we are in the process of applying for welfare.

Surely, something must be done. I have heard people speak about hope and a future that shall see the revival of some great Jewish literature, but rarely do they actively seek to awaken the renaissance. I have made my contribution, and so it is that I reach out to you. You have spoken about creativity. Indeed, you have made yourself clear about your longing, desire or passion for the arts of our people. This is why I have contacted you.

My family and I are not going to be just another sad, sarcastic statistic, no. Is the Jewish tradition the history of my family? Is it a triumph of evil? Is absurdity and misunderstanding our gods?

I don't know what else to say or do. I pray to G-d, but my prayers go unanswered; and these are returned to silence. My family came to America to build a life, not to end where they had begun.

I hope that this letter finds you, and is found well.

The letter was written before my father's suicide, which took place some time after my seventeenth birthday. I had no desire to reread the rejection letter, though having done so would have not been too different from what the class ultimately ended up doing. The next forty-five minutes were spent going over class policy and the student's handbook of proper rules and appropriate punishments, should one violate those rules.

Once class had ended, I went in search of my locker. Not knowing my way about the hallways, I asked the two students closest to me; two girls making conversation by their lockers, one leaning against, the other rummaging through.

"Hi. Do you know—" I stopped, I had to have another look at the paper which informed me of the number; "—where I can find Locker 218?"

The reply I received was almost automatic in time, dragging in tone, almost indescribably impatient in nature, "Are you retarded?"

The second response from her companion was little different, fingering ahead of me, "It's right there, *blind—*"

"Thank you," I said, moving myself quietly but quickly away from them, towards my locker. Depositing my things, being certain of the lock and locker combination, I was slowly becoming increasingly disorientated; the noise in the hallway was excessive, ricocheting from off the cornered walls, appearing to echo tunes from hell's own harp.

I went to the nearest bathroom, and there splashed my face with cold water, repeating this action at least three times. Taking a handkerchief from my waistcoat, I wiped my face dry, staring into the vanity mirror as I did this. Looking carefully at its lower left segment, I saw my stolen book in the urinal—! Coming closer to inspect it, its silver pages were now gold, the truth behind each dream of every alchemist. I took my food from out of my lunch bag, placed it into one of the numerous miscellaneous compartments of my backpack, for with it now I had this as for burial shroud, so then with a thick layer of paper with the accustomed purpose of toiletry secured, wrapped around my hands as glove, I, then, began, in turn, to carefully wrap my hands around the book, the skin not far from being impressed with the corrupted gold oozing from deep underneath it. With a filthy firm of reticence for grip, the book cocooned in its newfound shroud of burial, this dismal deed of multiple disgust done, I picked up the book, and gave it a proper burial as it were itself an image taken directly from my future in the gymnasium: I threw it into a dumpster on my way out from the boys' bathroom.

Returning to the hallway, not so much as a minute had passed before yet another pupil, this time husky and babyish, approached me; his eyes set on confrontation, but somehow lazy and lingering.

He was quick with his question, "Hey, you! Is your name *Keith*—?"

"It's Akeiden," I said.

"Like I care," he mumbled, then continuing, "I heard you harassed a friend of mine in the cafeteria."

"What?" I exclaimed with disbelief.

"Jasmine Williams, the girl who you were basically intent on seducing!" he exclaimed.

"I just asked her what she was reading!"

"Look *mate;* don't think you can spin me around little bunny-trapping circles: is that a good book, let's go book reading in the same library, I think we have the same chemistry class. I can't believe your nerve, you beer-barfing Scot?"

"My accent's English."

"Shut up!" Moving on ahead, he gave me his ultimatum: "You leave her alone or your gonna' to answer to me."

"Sure. Can I go now, *Cerberus*?"

To which he blatantly replied, "Yah, you can."

The bell was about to ring, and already the wheel came full turn. I went directly to my next classroom, hoping against hope to find some solace or satisfaction in this next round of tedious, repetitious instructions.

True to my accustomed inclination, I secured a seat that met the criteria that its predecessor had, though there weren't many other places to sit. Sitting myself down two seats from the window, my attempt was to savour these few remaining minutes before the same old session begins again. There was a kind of slowness in all this, but what I was experiencing now was not what I had experienced once at my last gymnasium, the private one. No. I sat in a room, listening how the wasting of the hours might come; for it was the hour of the homeless. The experience wrote a book; and it was not boredom that was its principal subject matter, but a dragging listlessness, if not a kind of lifelessness, which was to play no one the fool. This is the wounding stillness of high school chaos. It was obvious, if not desperately so; I wasn't going to learn anything, except the unnecessary: the avoidable.

Temporarily diverting my gaze towards the door, I happened to see a student with a pencil in his mouth enter the classroom, sporting his spectacles atop his forehead. Having seen what sat inside, he gave a tortured facial expression of exhaustion, impressing upon himself the need to quiet some pain, in order to endure the ensuing session. He sat down at the front of the class, setting his notebook atop the desk, and resuming to fidget with his pencil, his spectacles pocketed away, he continued appearing to quietly accept the social situation in which he was now in, but like me, I imagined, did not wish to be in. I took out one of my surviving books, which apparently hadn't yet been bored, and began reading.

Some more students entered, but this time they brought with them only disagreeable dispositions; one was greeted by the name Damon, but soon began to be addressed as Dan. I overheard their conversations, obscene pitiful testaments to the use of the language. I do not wish to write down what it is that I heard, but the matters with which they had concerned themselves was vacations abroad, staying up late in order to do more than your average student intercourse, and committing to forgetfulness the names of all whom you called *lover*. The three of them wished to sit where they pleased, and since sitting at the front of the class wasn't an option, two took seats to my immediate horizontal left, and the third, their leader, who I now realized was the bloody thief who stole my book; his clothes matching what I saw earlier, stood himself before my desk, looking down on me, as if I were some miscellaneous scum stuck on the heel of one of his old jogging shoes.

He addressed me accordingly, "It's time to start wandering, Jew."

"Look," my tired voice was probably dragging itself now, "it's the first day of school, and unless we're back in little grade school, I don't see how there can be arranged seating."

He hadn't listened to a single word I said, his reply being automatic, "It's mine, Jew. Now go back to Pharaoh!" This remark apparently had its intended affect on the two brainless donkeys, which seemed to burp their laughter, much like two moaning mules being struck.

His childishness had finally struck a nerve, and my reply came swiftly, "I don't see your name written on crayons anywhere on it, Danny boy!"

"Listen, Jew—"

"If you're in anyway smart," one of his friends interjected, "you'll do what you Jews are good at, and that's moving."

His fellow reiterating, "Be reasonable, and don't make it anymore difficult."

I had had enough; "I'll give you three some more advanced advice, and if you're an inch of a fraction smart, you'll just might get it: "Better to die in ash, than to carry the rifle with the bullet."

This response brought Damon's hand; he threw my book on the floor. After rising from my chair, asking what was his problem, he simply said that I was and shoved me back, after which I did the same. When I gave the second shove, a student exclaimed that the teacher was coming, and forthwith she entered. The lady gave me the impression that she could have been sitting on a goldmine, and rather than digging for the buried treasure, she just thought about gold. I took another seat, after insulting him, sat down, and tossed my backpack atop the desk: sighing angrily, disbelieving what was happening now. The seat I'd taken was just one half-seat behind, since they had been placed asymmetrically, on the opposite right-hand row, of . . . I couldn't believe it. The student who came in with a pencil in his mouth was looking at me;

I wasn't able to decipher his expression, but it appeared more involved than amused.

My response was almost immediate, "Leave me alone!" He turned his head grinning, and my head began receiving miniature-sized, notebook paper spit balls from the back of the class. I dug my head into my backpack, not believing, or refusing to believe, what was happening to me.

When the bell finally signalled our emancipation, it was lunchtime. I wanted to be alone, trying my best to invite some quiet back into my life; so I sat down by myself on a lone bench, next a flight of stairs, overlooking much of the school's edifice and surrounding natural landscape.

I wasn't hungry, but I was starving for some solace, an end to rapid havoc in the hallways. I just began meditating on how I had conducted myself, at times, with such slow movements, or some such sort of imperceptible gesture, which might have expressed either my melancholy or impoverishment. I was downtrodden, I had to have admitted that; but I didn't want to look the part, giving those callous cowards the pleasure of them seeing my perturbed frame of mind.

I did not move from my lonely sitting corner atop the bench, thinking a little about my old school. I had to leave this place, at least for now, by consigning myself to an act of imagination, resurrecting the past which now became more pressing than the immediate present. The mental landscape I was about to traverse was arduous, but I wished to sojourn, no matter the violence that had been done to my family, during my last school year there, when my father lost his job, and ended his life.

It was all the more familiar to me still, like a name. Longing was the means by which I would rouse, to have awakened my sleepy memories of the old school. Give me some respite from this . . . I thought to myself, if my reminiscing also came to nothing, like today's experiences, perhaps it was my *name*–who I am–that was at fault. If those memories do come back, reawakening how I was by nature: calm, courteous and collective; they would then be words, which would begin breathing air into old experience that might have been laid waste by time. Their sleep–so I should maintain–a kind of childhood folklore, a distance, which now having been subsumed by some nasty chaos, so much nonsense, had threatened the edifice of my previous adolescent fortune in being privately schooled.

I drew my attention to an act of concentration, asking peace to please reply to me, and I shall in turn reply to your reply. I didn't like being nostalgic, but I did not apologise for becoming nostalgic at such times as these, being as early as it was in the year; but time is a luxury I could no longer afford. I was not that rich, and probably never have been, though I might have thought myself as once having been, but . . . that is memory, and hence can no longer be.

I wasn't able to concentrate, though, with all that repulsive noise emanating from the cafeteria. *What were they doing in there*, eating the animal or butchering it?

The library was closed, and sheltered so much of the impossible; and as I had little choice to listen to my peers: I wandered through the echo, their resonance a bad habit that couldn't be ignored. This was the quietest place to sit, and so I became gradually aware of its stranger qualities because though I was alone, I was situated where I could also see other kinds of loneliness. Hypocrisy is a very lonely house in which to live. But . . . the stage had already been set, and having taken my seat, there was no turning back.

My fellow students! Their words were fragile vessels, easily sunk by some whimsical act. I suspected also that these vessels carried below deck a certain kind of cargo, the importance of which was in traversing the rudeness of the sea, tallying the sight of the nearest regions, however distant: in brief, to escape from one deserted island to the next, never finding buried treasure, which was the object of their to-ing and fro-ing. In their controlled desperation for human contact, they willingly agreed to confuse a hideous reality with an attractive illusion.

I was by myself, and becoming anguished. Loneliness, however, was not nourishing, overwhelmingly, my sense of sadness; it owed its being to my awareness of a truth devoid of purpose. It is this that gave me deep dissatisfaction.

For them, this was certain: Silence was a monument to danger, the harbour of interlude was hollow, and the lighthouses desperately sought; only deepened in distance by necessity, but hardened by great desire. What's wrong with a little quiet? My fellow students treated it as a dog cares for fleas or fire hydrants, between which little distinction was drawn: either you scratched, as by targeting someone or something for your object of ridicule, or you peed in order to mark your territory, that is, establish certain routines with which to decorate the lunch hour, claiming ownership of a student, usually either by degradation or adulation. One such routine was, I *overheard*, holding periodic contests to see who could fill the surrounding air with the most of their stench, the delivery of which I need not recount as it is of no great demand on the reader to imagine what it was. The original thought that I was entertaining at the time was a certain notion concerning loss, its content simply beginning, but lost due to what was happening.

If many of these students did actually harbour precaution, the instrument of prevention, which would prescribe them some workable knowledge, so as to locate these piers that they sought; it could be more to their good than danger. Loneliness and silence were the deep-sea monsters lurking below the shallow surface of the social waters. Would any have a peering eye to this false idea, or arid possibility? I very much doubt it.

Locked away from them, my book and I were lonely . . . I wanted to read but couldn't secure concrete contemplations, and so the book was without the reader and likewise I was without the book . . . but I was ensured by my patience that I would come to port, whereas a broken compass and false maps, its pantheon of self-same uncertainties, would guide theirs'; I wasn't going to slaughter my serene disposition so that I could secure some idle pastime: ridiculous! Their apparent need to nourish their loneliness with artificial companionships was of no new consequence to me: especially when I observed their conduct to its culmination.

I would later learn, unfortunately, that classes were no different. My studies were purely a waste of time. I wanted to study in earnest, at a private school. I had ideas. Originality was my great love; I had no need, let alone want, for some disgusting kind of dogmatism. Acknowledging what I later learned, my hunger became indistinguishable from necessity.

Society would heave me with an answer of how fabulous the invention of the public institution was. Being temperate to the opinions of others, I pursued the matter further. That it is a healthful means of educating our minds, a most excellent little get-together to dish up choice friendships: be social, learn things, do things, prepare for things, no doubt at all about that; a life lived without being schooled has missed a great opportunity, yes, certainly; but they would disguise the theme of their matter. For me it was quite the contrary. The purpose of school–as we have it now–was not apparent to me at all, never has been. And nor might it ever be, for in having the nature that I have always already had, I find public schooling as a means by which to simply teach itself how to become progressively unnecessary. Your point in being here is to prepare for life, not the virture-violating senior prom, or the like rubbish.

Schooling was an educational fasting. It borders on starvation, while overlooking absurdity; becoming absurd, and yet what is worse–than any other of its morose monstrosities–is the awareness it subverts to an alarming fact: a perception which diseases the consciousness with portent, and ominous philosophies. For as one suffers thus, in the confines of a school history, sufferings come, while others like mine end, and begin by being forgotten all over again; the nightmare situation is continuous. But especially by the forgers of the system, of whose true and disturbing nature most know nothing. Many are, also, simply ignorant of the truth, whether this is by intent or by accident (perhaps both), propelling us to carry deep within ourselves the passports to self-effacing parody. This is institutionalising, exposure to the abhorrent and monotonous.

I hear vulgar remarks from the stairway, something about cunningly injecting some more fun into the house that someone has just been invited to.

I break off from my thoughts, and observe my environment again. The birds were busy in beautifying their faces, occupied in an undercurrent of obsession, perfecting the vanity of appeasing themselves with eye-banquets, apocalypse, temporary surgeries, and the amendments of their physic. The distance did not obstruct my seeing the blokes remoulding their persons, idling in visual meanderings, gossiping without a code of self-restraint; they joked insidiously, peered at their peers as if they were possessions: obstacles, or just about anything other than Adam's descendants.

How punctual is the destruction of the human theatre, why all this play-acting? They had manufactured contradictions by the indefinite, progressively multiplying them.

I did not really desire to understand my peers, but I was left with little choice. Their hearts were honeycombs, and their social fictions were precious for them, and so they defended it in like manner to the drone. Painting over paintings, they were indeed busy.

The passer-bys. I soon found myself hearing, "I have to go" or "It's really getting late-", or some other such nonsense. I had rarely ever questioned, and nor did I find out, why some passer-bys, pressed with a question dealing with the time, for what o'clock it could have been; continued to act as if all was well. Why worry about time, when you don't really do anything with it? The concern was the of precious bejewelled bargain-brought brand-named illusions, spectral medallions in consciousness, certainly. And so caring nothing for it, my conduct was largely concerned in other things; such as how I had heard the voice of a teacher or student, what harmony had been meshed in with my ears, or how I had seen the face with which carried expressions, some polite, but distant, and others like my own. However, I found none that were my own right now.

Fading back into myself, my morning stroll to school was, fortunately, serene. I needed to summon substantial strength to withstand the "Home of the Phoenixes", and such resource was soon becoming scarce, an emptying account. The illusion around me was cold, but for those whom are cradled and comforted by it, it is similar to the warmth received by the hand, when it is outstretched near open fire, which shields the senses from nature's less celebrated affections. The human mind is naturally drunk with dreams, but being sobered, longing dethrones the fresher airs of invention, and rekindles imagination's enlightenment, a truer fire with which to deal with life. The illusion isn't necessarily apparent sometimes. It is so inconstant that even when I can still see the students, like books at night by candlelight, books which are nearly hid in darkness, so too is the illusion nearly equally hid. My peers began lusting over various excitements, thinking carefully about not thinking carefully about the content of their actions. Their social bonfire intricately illuminates, casting shadows that intertwine like finely woven spider webs. A collective despair.

Tired of people, I began to observe a tree in the distance, a solitary. Dear nature's smile, elegant in its presentation, but perfectly blemished in its actualisation, which is the counterpart. I concentrated my strain of thought on this tree, looking carefully at how the leaves were being rustled, my attempt simple; to find harmony by gesturing imagination in its natural motions—to whichever gesture with which I might have communicated to myself my situation. I must learn from nature directly, sometimes. For even the simple act of saying hello to someone I had known, in previous "lifetimes", was a delicate matter; especially since I did not care to turn the greeting into a circus, a circus for the general performance of many weird stunts, and the like displays of accordant aberrations: such numerous eccentric creatures. A few leaves fell, throwing my attention off focus.

I hear gossip in the background. Gossip is intolerable. I do not want to hear any of it. This was my same reaction to swearing; I did not want to hear it but had to have gone and use it. With very little fanfare, none of these two wishes, which I held up to sincerity by observing them during my tenure at the good school, had been embraced by oblivion while I sojourned at "The Home of the Phoenixes" and so the golden age had drawn to a close.

I interrupted myself; it was then I called for the construction of my vision. I silenced thought, and voiced stillness: looking at the tree, again. Here in this school the academic endeavour was as complex as it was also annoyingly stupid, but it wasn't. Here I was, to build something sizable and magnificent perhaps, a monument, a construction that is precious; for I have blessed it with my capacity to create, that is, to monument my mind that I might be able to produce something in the image of nature, divine harmony, and what was it that I did: re-enact the Middle Ages within myself. There is no spiritual splendour in any of this. I am unable to draw clear distinctions: the students have confused sensuality for sexuality, an unfortunate intercourse; have orphaned virtuousness for adopting viciousness, a tortured psychology; but worse is their thinking they have crushed ubiquity by temporality, doing everything by doing nothing! What am I doing, presently? What am I doing dallying with sad sacks who did–no doubt–try to destroy in an hour what they themselves could not do in a lifetime? The prospect was simply disgusting, and it was at this point that I was tempted to give it to nothing; and persevere the work solely to myself, for myself. When I had been apparently decided to do this, however, to effectively abandon my work until such a time that I may deem it ready to return to it, I realised just how much my work might mean to someone who I do not know, have not known, nor will I ever know. I knew my family loved me if only for the fact that in the construction of their affection they could appreciate the integrity as well as the intricacy of the person, whom they loved–they thought–so selflessly, but it started and finished with blood bounds. You're born in blood, and they love you because of it. Perhaps, those few friendships that I now do not yet have, or may indeed never possess, shall be brought about by my work; or is it simply my duty to do the work for, as a certain sage said, we are not free to desist from it? I have intelligence, so I might use it.

Thinking about it, seeing that old anonymous maple tree shaped like some senior citizen imposing his weight on the walking stick; I became aware of how exactly downcast I was; the details seem to be as new to me, as they may be to you. The resemblances I have to these remembrances are precarious. I see how I shall end because my beginning is that point of the future at which I shall be taught endings—

The bell has rung, causing a flood of faces and failures to ensue. Those daft Nimrods, the other Nicks and Joshes, my athletic class, the bell and its bloody incessant ringing, lunch interludes, crowds of students hurrying, hasting the hours, hastening away at their hammering and being hammered; its silence with their stentorian marches of the mouth—the bell rings, thus begins the cycle all over again.

I was walking down a hallway; I saw students painting their faces with laughter: in my mind I wanted to read a book, but the library . . . has closed. It must open now, no; the last bell rings, so began history class.

I sat myself down, near me was an old window enclosed in a more hallow wall. There's a cornucopia of chairs laid before me, looking out the window; this window which presented its view before my sleepy vision, is!—

The instructor has wisely chosen his subject because he repeats well, if not too well, what has already been said: so I went to the provinces of imperial repetition, cycles laid waste on cycles. A few more classes done, I was soon to begin athletics.

My physical education instruction was–so experience says–an introduction to the confraternity of the immaculate obsession: a painfully ambiguous index of prioritised illusions. Nature dictates the mind to invite the constitution to partake in its prosperity, thus establishing equilibrium between the two. But should this mutual understanding be ignored, its precepts committed to forgetfulness, then profound discharges of the quietly deranged shall–so I should reveal–come to dictate by its presence the absence of the harmonious.

My experience here contradicted the long held and established truth, giving this instead: we have sacrificed the stillness of the mind for the unnatural violence of the body. The muscles we marshal mean as much to universal health as, say, the riches of thieves to property, when its principle is called upon to justify the unjustifiable. It's theft.

Athletics, all during P.E.! I was sick of stealing; and so when the class was over, I returned to the boys' locker room with much conspicuous chaos in my conscience.

Sweating, spitting, swearing, and stealing deluged the corresponding senses with its befouling excess. The sudden streams of conversation were all around me; as I prepared to undress, the words spoken heretofore had long regress, digressed, and impressed upon their listeners naked aspects of the lies they had already busied themselves in telling. I simply wanted to be done with it, waiting anxiously for the dismissal bell to bring the tired school day to an end.

I was about to take off my shirt, when, quite suddenly, Damon approached me, saying, "Hey, Jew!"

I refused to turn around, owing to my embarrassment of the situation; I did not wish to wake myself to the reality of the ensuing ridiculousness.

"I thought you weren't afraid of me," he challenged.

"I'm not, you daft philistine," I answered.

This response warranted my person being shoved, according to which act I shoved back, calling him some additional obscene insult.

Suddenly, when I was to be shoved twice, a voice exclaimed, saying: "Damon, what the . . . !" The same student who came into the class with that tired expression, who was looking at me after the first encounter, was now staring Damon in the face, refusing to break eye contact with him.

"Lay off, Hesch! This has nothing to do with you." Damon was becoming noticeably nervous now, his erect posture an obvious sham, as were his words which were devoid of any actual confidence now.

"Oh, but I think it does. Why can't you ever match your actions with some of the words you mouth? How about fighting someone who stacks up against you for a change, huh?" Finishing the remark, his taunting posture and facial countenance boomed with a burning authenticity, his message punctuated with conviction.

"I'll fight you, but not here," said Damon, desperately intimated. He then turned his back on him, so as to simply walk away from the situation, some laughter in the background. Heschel was afire with insult, and he too turned round, then spat on Dan's head. Hesch was inspecting and imposing, his demeanour determined and disgusted.

"If you're ready to fight him here, you can fight me now," he challenged.

"Alright," Damon said reticently.

A fight ensued, with Dan and Hesch circling each other with their fists raised, the air intoxicated with want for the struggle. Hesch was quick to strike Dan's face first, the students becoming hungrier and louder for casual carnage, free in their ferociously fresh desire to observe public exhibitions of the frenzied. Their movements were more instinctual than instructional, a few reactions on Dan's part resulted in Hesch's lower lip being struck, but he was quick to injure his opponent badly; and now exhausted on the floor, Hesch picked up Damon's head and slammed his face against a wooden bench. Dan's nose was broken, and Hesch fell back a little, reclining tiredly against the red shower walls in the locker room. Dan's face stared down, placing his hand in order to capture some of the blood gushing from out his nostrils. The red pool beneath his face was . . .

The whole experience was soon over, and the coach, after enjoying some of the spectacle for himself sent the both of them presumably to the head office, suspension sure to follow.

One class left, and all during that period I thought about one thing alone: the locker room confrontation, its eventual struggle. I didn't listen to anything the teacher said, my thoughts singularly concentrated on that one event. It was such that when the dismissal bell had rung, I secured my things, beginning my exodus from the gymnasium, as if I had wakened from a strangely inviting but disturbingly intricate nightmare. I had no desire to take the school bus, preferring instead to walk the discrete distance back home, it not even being half of half a mile.

The inconstant wind, these afternoon breezes, meshed almost imperceptibly with the echo of my footsteps, and finding myself deluged with profound disappointments, I began to contemplate once more the edifice of today's experiences.

Homesickness became my natural stream of consciousness. Its gradual growth marked a motionlessness of my soul, a destruction of sacred things: to silence prayers by a false witness to their destruction; I was rebuilt to understand how the necessities of production were to have by my departments a handbook performance. I missed my old boarding school in England, and my awareness of my missing it appeared to define how I had experienced what had happened at school today.

I was, initially, little conscious of this; but . . . I was fastened to a sure succession of sorrow from which I could not unbind myself. It was this listlessness—a motionlessness of my mind—that later became, as I began to venture deeper into the dark corners of the year, a door to my own destruction. Malnourishment, mayhem, malformation, misshapenness, and mediocrity are its princely manifestations: these all lead to nowhere, but public schooling is the past master in getting you there, and fast.

I was struck by how melancholy–moved I was, but then again, three successive years of public schooling had begun to surface from the deep, awakening the mind to its intoxicating discontent—to be infinitely drunk with woe.

I did not seek this, but I had found it as much as it had found me. Disaster comes uninvited, but not necessarily unexpected; it is insidious so that sometimes I think the history of the world is crammed by this experience into my school years, preparing me to ready its larger lessons. What devices, what instruments are these that they may engineer that which I thought impassable impossible?

There's no script from which I could read these things, what audience, friends or family, but a desert, my solitary self, this being a final gesture among the lost to signal hope in life's dangerous simplicities.

Walking home, my ability to assess the day's tapestry, to see finely its fabrics, intricacies, cleverness, patterns and material narration, was a death to my sense of patience; it waned like a reluctant kiss to a ready recipient, becoming gradually insubstantial, and if I could do this: recall what has happened with patience, it'll be like raising from the dead a newer corpse to be old-time devoured.

There was no return. I thought to myself: "Now I suffer whatever it is that I am meant to suffer." The rocky terrain of an isolated wilderness was my lot, is my lot, but what I suffered did not have to be allotted to me; this vein of revelation still lingers in my soul, an acid stillness that does not move. There is no solution, but a resolution to look truth in the face and accept it, coldly, cogently, faithfully.

The sentence, if it was indeed a sentence, did not express a thought, but fought the incontrovertible against its self. It struck me more in the nature of a shout, more than anything else, my quiet thoughts; remembering the bell ringing, our sessions begun or ended, all was excavating the artefacts of my fears. It was like some great fire whose spark could not be wrenched asunder, so as to breed initial density into unconventional difficulty, complex impossibility.

A lonely traveller, surely if any recourse to either sign or symbol had been called upon to serve the understanding, that is the image I would call upon in order to do justice.

But what understanding? The nature and extent to which that disservice rose struggled against incredulity–my senses have been thus impressed. As my thoughts became more realised, I proceeded to take my instructions, feeling *misery* without trying to convince myself that I wasn't. To my preconceived malcontent, this justified doom; these melancholy constructions appeared to have been as high as summits, deeper than seas, saltier than tears, which now fallen, continue to inflame the passions into infernal desperations: the gentler hell of suffering and suffering alone.

There seemed to yet remain denser deepness in my consciousness to no end. The intricate disposition of common practice was–to my mind–making excess. Mazy and dizzying, upon the slope of evergreen envy for some past that did not exist; I was observing the cornucopias of domesticated real estate, all of which were laid like the labyrinthine before me.

I was numbed by the time I returned home; climbing the outdoor stairs, refusing to study the decorations my mother had put atop the patio, I hastened my hand to unlock the door, impatient to reclaim the serenity I had lost by attending the gymnasium.

No one awaited me; with all our savings spent in order to buy this house, my mother worked with indifference to the clock, so by the time she came home I was long gone—fast asleep.

Shutting the door, flinging my backpack on the kitchen table, I pulled a chair and began attempting to steady the stream of anger and anxiety swelling up deep inside me. I couldn't believe what a terrible, monotonous day this had actually been.

"At home, alone . . . thinking about school," I thought to myself.

Reclining on the kitchen chair, tilting my head backwards a little, I began to stare at various lithographs depicting Sephardic history hung from the wall.

The first lithograph depicted a Sephardic synagogue, empty and immense. The second depicted a solitary scholar standing before ruins, lamenting over the loss of the synagogue; presumably, I imagined, from the first lithograph.

That nagging sense just refused to go away: school, school, school . . .

I believed once that hell was some god-forsaken pit in the hungry belly of imagination: a distant place to be found nowhere on earth; but what had happened to me today contradicted this. Missing the school bus this morning was unwelcoming enough, but the events which followed had continued to upset, disturbing a daunting variety of memories, fears, beliefs, desires, affections, passions, the appalling complexity of which had already been fragile to begin with.

A tortured knowledge has slithered into the chasms of consciousness; and being thus, I now know not anything else. But . . . what I may ask of myself is to persist in the struggle, as a bird–which being wounded–might do, when it persists to sing songs in an insecure forest. The little wounded bird, capable of such tenacity, may do well, though aware of nature's inclination to violent suddenness, which shall be named ignorant by impersonal forces; especially since not too far into the surrounding spaces, there lies a coiled serpent ready to strike at it. It is possible that in a like blending of events, over which uncertainty has dominance, the armies prepared for blood, bondage, and battle's bounty shall do no differently to me. High school was that serpent, and the songs sung by the bleeding bird but telltale traces of where to find it so that it might destroy it.

As is often the case, the war against which I have fought, I am also its soul; this is more a torment of boredom, rather than an evolution of excitement. Time is analogous to a dream, and desire, by whatever degree, therein. Want is in these camps, a prelude inception. I imagine peace in order to escape from its counterpart, which are no more real than emotions imposed upon us by dreaming. I imagine a distant landscape, a weeping welkin, flooding confluence: nature's perpetual revolution measures true to peaceful expectations. Continuing to soothe my frame of mind by contemplating in this vein, time resolves and dissolves itself into a puzzle of serendipity, as a dream. Want, need, an ambition and accordant actions have begun to constitute a surfacing tranquility upon the waters of emotion.

A sudden thought courses through my mind, reminding me of the Jewish artwork; they are gifts from the family, commemorating my Bar Mitzvah.

The thirteenth year is traditionally observed in Jewish life as the eastern direction, where a true adulthood is dawned: achieved in Jewish men and women. Whether or not the tragedies of my seventeenth year were inevitable, a patterned puzzle secretly hidden in nature, does not take away the fond memories I had, and continue to have had, when I reflect on the joy of my being Bar Mitzvah. The celebration was without the stock of the whimsical children because I prepared well for this festive occasion.

It was, also, at this time that I had taken great interest in the principles of the industrial sciences. In architecture, the activities I most admired were drawing and designing: in their interactions, systems, the abolitions and reintroductions of the frameworks; and in a general supervision of the actual construction, such like subject matter, is where the human mind works most like

G-d. This reality was simply too tasteful to my intellect to afford any possible resistance at all.

Unlike, however, the First in Eden, the argument, which held me strongly in support, was the fact that I knew that G-d did what I had done: that we were creators, whereas with the First–certainly–they did not know whether or not G-d himself had tasted of the Forbidden Fruit; any opinion in this matter was simply that: opinion. Inclusion was an inclination in paradise, so the story contends. Temptation: a misinterpretation of obedience. Adam and Eve must have wanted to do what all cultured children say they want to do, especially when in profound admiration of their parents. Do they not say, "When I'm grown up, I want to be just like you."

Maturity for the mind means questioning, at least in part. This developing characteristic of our nature is prime for cultivating a rebellious consciousness—an informed attitude. But too much, even in good spirit, is dangerous. Excess is one of the original monsters of the Creation. Furthermore, rebellion was the primal theme of their burgeoning existence, a disagreeable necessity which–if avoidable–should be avoided. For the most part, if we are to believe certain dogmas, G-d was made out to be the crusher of rebellions, reminiscent of the bureaucratic: the ancient Orient potentate. He who has unchallenged dominion over the providence, prosperity, and property of his subjects; it is in this light that makes us little more than slaves, feeble foibles in gratuitous masquerades, maliciously mocking freedom's truly distant dimensions, implications, sense, intricacy, and actualisation. The G-d of Abraham who has patience for when he is challenged, someone whom may be argued with, speaks to me; the G-d of Isaac who is mysterious, moves me; the G-d of Jacob, he who wrestles with his creation, pleases me; but the G-d of Moses–who is the crusher of bureaucrats, sycophants, tyrants, and the like–simply fascinates me; but even more importantly, he convinces *who I am*. The unrighteous by reason of their despotisms are demolished, though time is usually subtle in this way. No hurry on G-d's part then! This is the G-d of the People. Thinking thus, continuing many like contemplations, I drew a habit of identifying the Creator as the Defender.

I remember my speech, or rather, what few additional thoughts I added to the speech. For this is what I said when I was Bar Mitzvah, and it was what I felt when I began thinking about a past pupil.

There was a student in my old school who approached me after he'd learned that one of his friends, who had betrayed his trust, had told me about his conversion from Judaism to Christianity. I did not wish to know this, but I too was fooled; the betrayer of the betrayer said he needed to talk to me about the class assignment, so when we met, he blurted his friend's act to me.

Within days, the convert confronted me. I wasn't really pleased to see him, especially when I consider the fact that he was a noted anti-Semite. I haven't forgotten our little chat:

"I knew you would soon know what I once was," he said, wrenching the words asunder with aversion.

"What do you want, Michael?" I said, maintaining a patient countenance.

"An answer to a question."

"I am listening."

Throwing his gaze round the room, his posture clearly mangled by unease, he continued, "I was born what I was, as so were you; but I broke free from my birth-chains, as you haven't. Why?"

"I am Jewish; that is my explanation," refusing to indulge my sense of aggravation.

"Don't be an idiot—"

Waving my hand much in the way a judge would upon passing sentence, I said, "Now that's interesting, for that was the word I came to associate with you, in one form or another."

"Ironic?"

"No, it is not."

"Then what?" he asked puzzled as he was annoyed.

"Perverse."

Hearing my response, he became angry, saying, "The Jews are their own victims; the Jews are doomed unless they show the strength they showed in the Old Testament!"

To which I replied, "All beginnings have as their shadows the inevitabilities of endings. As for such stuff as the strength we have read in the Tanach, it is the virtue all must muster in order to endure the dangerous, less error consumed them."

"Are you attempting to correct my beliefs or me, Akeiden?"

"What one believes is what one is, for faith in whatever form it assumes informs our decisions. But your beliefs are not beliefs, Michael."

His face disfigured by confusion, sweat dripping faintly from off his forehead, he shot me his next question, "What, then?"

"They are illusions to the justification of the unjustifiable; it is that simple."

I began walking away, when I heard him call from the distance, "Akeiden, I know there are truths in fictions the likes of which eclipse equally the time!"

Having recalled this exchange also excavates fresh memories of what had happened this morning in school: being accused of deicide and sexual harassment. And like then, as now, I found solace in nature.

The middle-aged afternoon was hauntingly clear, the object of my words, as well as its ideas, were equally brimming in all their utilities. My understanding has been separated into two many divisions like lands split by general fractures, fancies, and particular frenzies, which also may be mere illusions.

I continued steadfast into these unquiet moments of repose, reflecting like the moon.

I decided to make myself a cup of tea . . . waiting a few minutes, then drinking slowly . . . thinking less.

To reflect on the past is to stand in the shadows, eternity being that shadow. I arose from the chair, pulled myself to the window . . . had to have my eye spectacles repositioned, each hand adjusting its opposite ends, and directed my gaze towards the roof. I saw some light twinkling atop a roof corner, most of the ceiling was gone; and the darkness brought by the fallout had yet to obstruct it. I'm remembering the house I grew up in; it was bought quickly and bulldozed quietly.

Distant childhood memories crawl from out the woodworks, and one-eyed nostalgia shall then play the woodpecker.

To remember the past means to sacrifice the present, so as to put future on the altar of forgetfulness. How many mornings had I woken to, to hear dad cleaning out the gutters.

The landscape of my old neighbourhood was mountainous; now it's costal. Looking out the window, I am reminded of how much has changed, but not for the better.

I looked at the lithograph depicting the solitary scholar again, a Jew lamenting the loss of the synagogue.

Examining the piece by calling upon the instrument which made it possible, the imagination, I began to envisage how he might have prayed in the temple; that is, seeing how he saw that which has now been taken away from him.

I imagine . . . praying; the worshipper prayed for the suffering, those in need. But would those for whom he prayed now begin to pray for him? His wrinkled face filled with intention, the curve of the cheeks and depth of the lines, while expressing his anguish, were not so much as ambiguous as it had been strangely apparent. The spectator did not need to see his tears in order to know his soul was being overwhelmed by lamentation. His loudest expression of grief? Silence.

He clasps his hands, crushing his knuckles inward and lifting them; he shields his eyes away from the calamity. His face buried thus, his sacred garb is contorted according to the anguished position of the body.

The scholar is soliciting the object of devotion for redemption. His sunken posture emphasizes the habit he has had to desire for a finely woven thread of perplexity, the mysterious ways of his God are now alien to him; he's been estranged from eternity, the mansion in which the deity dwells. He thought he believed he had understood the sufferings of others, but having his, he is now incapable of even understanding himself. His purposes are now lamentable, to carry on, a source from which he seeks to overthrow justice by instituting reason, and so he gambles not entirely unwisely.

The lithograph has captured the hateful harmony of survival; the tortured perspective and dark coloured features all testify to an irredeemable pain. This negative theme is supported by my visual appreciation; seeing the illustration for what it is, I cannot counter the argument of the artwork. The consequence of my characterization marks the distance, between redemption and annihilation, little spaces in between. How to redeem is barely possible unless there are spaces to the augmentation of their interludes, in order to prevent the development of the demonic, which is not necessarily evil in any traditional sense.

The solitary scholar was–in the judgement of the judges–as equally misplaced, as I thought his aggressors misshapen disturbances. The victim is lost, but not so much as his attackers. How much evil is actually born of good, and good evil, disturbs me. The lithograph hanging from the kitchen walls is a testament to this complex calamity. The possibility is somehow strangely distant to my original perspective of it; I am made enfeebled, harkened to hate when I think of his enemies; much like our minds are when they are dallied by the stretching out of duration. The body ages, no matter how indifferent to and/or ignorant of time we are, as does the mind by practical disorder, that is, chaos that benefits some, but condemns the many. The primary implements with which this chaotic construction occurs, is occasioned by means of a general inclination in the politic, whispers whispered: as if amongst thieves, or distrusting lovers.

Observing a certain juxtaposition, the one lithograph as against the other, a temple with and worshipper without, bring to mind yet another theme in the illustrations. History is its parody; its unwritten history is its tragedy. The worshipper prayed for people in distant places, whose faces he does not know nor whose voice he shall ever hear, and while he might have certainly prayed for those in his constituency; it was fear, the prayer of the unconscious, which remains, and is a remainder thus. So, goes the order of chaos.

The nature of this dangerous design, this profoundly enigmatic–if not absolutely absurd–anguish, is manufactured with precision, distributed exactingly; realitied with as much certainty, I fear, as there is in the certitude of our deaths.

I sensed almost that the initial distress of the lamenting Jew is given way, torn down, held back, pushed aside: thus dissuaded by dismissal; this is the purpose of a certain ignorance, to ignore pain and the sophistication of evil. The greater evil, sometimes, is when it is ignored. For this made firm in their forms only after having been fixed in either ignorance or naivety, not realising how evil actually is.

Such sickness negates neither the laws of our heart, nor necessarily the play-acting of its art, no; but rather it frustrates, initially, and internally the exteriority of the playacting wherewith such design is deceptively concentrated. It builds a Tower of Babel, to be like God, only to be banished from either the Tower, which is hope, or God, from whom hopelessness might have sprung. God couldn't change a generation, so he just had them drowned in Noah's flood. And what did Noah do, the most virtuous of his generation, after God promised he would never do this again, the threat of divine violence: he got drunk.

This is a difficult matter, a dense disharmony to lay waste by description. Disharmony is a risk of such design, and its price can become devastatingly apparent in its apparel of catastrophe.

The hidden tears of the solitary Jew are lyrics praising, communicating, lamenting; revealing: by such like speeches, unfortunately, what has been silenced, so as to lay waste the sense with which a desert might have been turned instead into a lush forest, rather than a desolate plain of grievous echoes.

It is rather simple this chaos. Its farmlands of old owe their yield to the weeds, a yet most keenly fouled growth. It's simply built up by them. One man's cure is another's man's disease, a love with which they make their hearts hardened, and hardening heartening. Time and blood are essential to their demonic formulas.

If there were unpleasantness in a second, such sadness in a minute, and still worse repulsion in the hour, how would I fare the fair length of a year? That prison-school wasn't going to lighten up, but get worse.

Such concerns house many minds: appetites are awakened, and they yearn–one way or another–to be fed. Their appetites are less than this as they are cries, an encyclopaedia of anguish to be detailed by need alone, so much for the subject of such books, never to be read.

The destroyers of the temple are absent from the lithograph, but the original engraver was sure to haunt the artwork with their presence. Not for the Jew-haters. Their hatred was naked, and sought no protective layers.

It was an edifice for all to see; and one, whom was to be admired or appalled, had to have known this. The victim is scarred by the attack, and his wounds are witnesses to the assault.

This simplicity is not, however, random. Its simplicity, no matter how it is brought about, entails a certain license for which an application lies in wait, an act of exacting justice; and the scholar shall now, while hiding his tortured gaze, become a solitary hunter prowling behind foliage; its target finely fitted into the frame of his field of vision. The gap between the fingers reveals this, I believe.

The uncertain future may make waste the idea for an ancestry in the civilisations that purposed themselves in making laws, and establishing houses for the sanctuary of their beliefs. A chance is taken when truth is revealed. The solitary scholar's ancestors built the temple, and their future enemies destroyed it . . . but God did allow it, if he so believes what the faith of his fathers teaches him. Having the means to make our ideas so, the surviving scholar, having subtle insight into the truth of things, just might proceed to make a metropolis of the person we think we know, a metropolis being a city of appalling complexities, sinister safety, and disturbing revelation into the nature of its chief architect.

The nature of pain is meticulous; it shares the precision of a spider spinning its web of finely woven silk, especially since its appearance is meant to betray its reality.

It is simple. This simplicity may elicit sympathy, or perhaps, one might even say interest. The interest might be nothing other than scholarly curiosity, a historian of ideas for want of precaution. But once done, there is some food for his appetite left, and that particular feature in him is an indefinite extent, the time in which he takes some samples, the savouring is infinite. Justice for such a scholar is not afraid of blood. It is now, usually, when his interests are stripped, and his predilections touched. History he believes is ripe, and the agriculture of deceit, against which he shall now fight, is replenished with a bounteous vessel of his vision, to which blindness is unclear, or at least, no more stable than are our memories at the instant in which we have fallen asleep. It seems to leave life merely as it was, an echo to its experience, reducing to simple dust all that had anything else, which might have had its intricate answer.

The cave of solitude, which being cavernous, is hollowed further by reluctance. He must act, a solitary, a specimen of nature's eremites, their structure: the instrument by which the echoes of the winds are shed, the place from which something precious has been stolen. The truth is known to us that what has been stolen can never be returned to us. How strange is this!

The surviving scholar depicted in the lithograph . . . yet he still waits for the arrival of his hope. He believes this to be unassailable, for him it is no less assured than his death. His hope had only been a desire, originally an insignificant chaos from which he had extracted a composition of some great order. This too became food for loss, however. Further to this, it had become spiritual recreation, a sort of licensed irrationality, however desperate, by which he might have imagined other things, anything else, in order to escape the purpose for which he had been chosen. But he had not misjudged, and having taken on additional dimensions, he was soon without such licence, let alone that desire, which had been after all, his singularly initiated drive, which would no longer propel him. He was free, but to pay the price for freedom from ignorance is costly, unbearable really. It usually requires bankruptcy.

Ignorance was over now, if not entirely. It's food for bittersweet sessions of nostalgic reflection, perhaps; those gradually loosening remembrances, which soon he had found little more than remainders of having been unable to find anything in the way of appeasement. It is this girth, more than anything else, that is his wallet: his faith, paid by his bankruptcy.

The wallet he carries at his back for some later forethought. Hope for him became a reason to which its continuation is, solely, the continuing of his predicament, useless. Hope distracts action, he believes. Sometimes, however, it is also necessary, so that he could sustain himself in later tribulations. So little goes into this, until it becomes something bordering on the instinctual.

No less emotion to express, I thought.

The detailed destruction of the sacred sanctuary, his little shul, is absent from the depiction. It is pain, his facial anguish, which alone wakens awareness to injustice. The presence of diseased minds and their thoughts sickened my mind; their hungers for conquest and the bloodied economies of its glories, starved me.

He's hungry now; the scholar is, for those quiet qualities inherent in its prized province. All these things in their unnatural dispositions were all executions, successive acts of deepening the silence. My soul had been lobed into this hell, and it would be done again in the martyring of ensuing school days: a day after day, from day to day and until the last of days.

There was a dictionary of emotion I had to define for when in defining them, I was gradually made aware, reawakened to my father's words; his single entry that carried round its scope the invaluable range and tangibility of his love for his family.

No longer was he a scholar at peace with himself, but anguished, impoverished. His only goal now is to rekindle the conflagration, and rescue justice from being idle food for maggots to excel their growth to flesh-eating worms.

Shall he take a risk to right the wrong? I imagine he grabs a stick of goodly height, with what I think may only be a white and pale complexion, and he sits on a rock of inevitability, which inhabits the mind alone. As he sits still, only then does he slowly begin to bend his left leg inward, and reclines on his right side with both arms. He seems dark and distant, but is hauntingly familiar to almost everyone, as an incarnate of a universal repose. His anguished contemplation is a brief moment, a small term served in the prison of time, for the human is incarcerated in a cell of fleeting glimpses, fragile moments that wisp away, leaving only a whisper in the violence of history. It is that fragile, but what he does will be unbreakable, never to be forgotten.

Retracting my observant eye from the lithograph, I inadvertently succeeded in doing much toil in my court's jurisdictions, by revealing the artwork's true nature. But there are some cases, which should have never been brought to court. I cannot, however, indulge ignorance, so I should withstand.

I leave the solitary Jew lamenting away; he does his waltz, a study of the sacred stillness haunting an anguished infinity, and I mine.

I am fond of relating to anyone my experiences of having been privately schooled, for it was the choicest education. To my mind, all else does but seem to have been well versed in death's paleness, in its poorly built mansion of compensation.

How it had all been reduced to rubble, a history made no differently from the temple or my house; it had been tossed amongst the heaps of broken dreams.

The healthful desire to do well, and the pale disease of worsening antagonism at not doing well, became my time and fate, a distance to traverse, a mighty sea on which the desire to return to land entails having to set sail, through fear, doubt, danger and disbelief. The journey is jagged and juiced in jeopardy, but to voyage against wind and water in order to do so, to go back, would then become a necessary obligation. These are the ripples of great change, awakening in me a realisation that has yet to come to fruition.

This truth, its inevitability as truth, had awakened in me, in my once relaxed awareness of the world, a sense of dread, and this was not necessarily at the truth, so much as it was with what was to come.

To this day, it is bewildering for me to understand why children waste their time, in familiarising themselves with folly, regret, and food for nostalgia. Still, I am sure that if kept in check, like any other uncultured habit, idle children may have their chances, later on in life.

This only proved me prophetic, especially since that particular instance of disrespect, in the classroom, hallways, cafeteria and need I say the boys' locker room, had been all but anticipated by me. I awoke from my dreary reflections–dreaming in a dusty bed, called time - the door opens, my hand pressing the knob tightly. I glimpse out into the neighbourhood streets. The swift wind is silent - blows the leaves, dreams of the sleeper.

I see a puddle or two. Little leaves, too. There's another. It falls into the reflecting waters of a nearby pond. That seems to break into streams that lead to a river. I needed to go for a walk, and began walking.

The soft strides with which I progressed towards the beach, they were relaxing and quieting.

The wind stroked softly against the hair, delicate movements like a mother's hands; the smooth flow of its harmonious melodies was quieting to the turbulent ebb and flow of dizzying emotion. It is a flirtation with the serene, each breeze the writing of numerous pens attempting to rewrite troubled feelings: scribbling, dabbling their work. Walking quietly from out the house, entering the street, and then making my way through grassy emptied lot, I realised the sure-successions of its compositional excellence; it was a note harder than the hardness of brute stones, a frozen emotional icescape.

The chattering of wind and thoughts was the breaking of a pencil against a rock, with each remembrance rekindling various episodes of a privileged childhood, which now have been lost. The taste of nostalgic wretchedness was thick in pleasure but thorny in pain, the significant difference between which was now slowly becoming lost.

Not too far from the old abandoned lighthouse, I continued walking towards the direction from which I heard the waves quietly wash ashore, then being sucked back into the ocean.

It was unexpected how I suddenly began thinking about Heschel, his expression when I first saw him. The dissatisfied youth clung to quietness like lonely clouds hung atop the celestial ceiling, some of which I now see gracing the sky above me. It was apt to be being pushed but remaining still; and were such a situation to occur, it would have meant having to vacant a "public execution house", as I would later describe it. This was the calm before the storm, as well as after it. The mood not distantly similar to when a soldier looks at his bloodied hands, lifting them in front of the face, floods of staining red which may prelude the pale future that is to be found only in death. How the engines of ruin persevere The student: a map of the world, a distance between civilization and annihilation, as I am for want of saying.

Judging by appearance all seemed too tolerable, if not remotely enjoyable; and yet yield-after-yield, the harvest returned more emptied, more desolated than it has ever been. I knew what I did not want to say. The classes were banal. The strangeness of school had all but dissipated, only to resurface tomorrow morning.

No, I'm not going to tolerate the trash, this poor excuse for wasting existence.

Devotion was sought in my solitude, thus deluging my mind with thought and doubt. The continuing circle . . . and in so doing I scraped the knees of my consciousness, by going back to school, should I choose to do so.

I think, "I know that in order to get an idea of the building, one must do more than merely study the foundations. The entire character of the constructor mustn't only be glimpsed, but also fully appreciated, apprehended: acquired. Teaching is one of the best ways of learning."

By slow and steady streams, the voice of the past is itself made into a whisper of the future, a temporal punctuation; unnecessary, as is death to the dead; but it was obliging to my disbelief, and difficult to my will, to permit the faculty, which we identify as memory, to operate sufficiently without resorting to disorder. Contemplating previous people and places, a misleadingly graceful gesture of nature's, nostalgia that is; I found myself overwhelmed by the sense of such nostalgic sessions.

It is this, more than anything else, which has created a sore in my soul, sickness which in turn has been diseased by nature, and worsened further by a few yet last nestled promises, all of which have been broken, but also of which the most prevalent is a process, and it is to this process I ascribed the most significant discrepancy which I have thus far observed. That is to say, the process of contradictions, such as hope, wherewith I have been made into that which I am: a seventeen-year-old teenager, a Jew, a European-raised Israeli-born Jew, whom has been asked by nature's creator to create, and to create creatively; if I am to bother myself in creating at all.

Those contents are only apparent to me now as the unbearable image of an unbearable sorrow, that of its infinite uncertainty to the rest of the edifice. This quality is like the dead dressed in their corpses, perfumed by some, if not by the many tears of the observers of Yahrzeit, for in remembering the lost, they are mourning theirs. These dead were lost in vein, and it is this particular quality of iniquity, which I hear echoing in Israelite history, call them the cries of innocence, that now lie lost. It is a child unborn whom is held by the hands of time.

Pain was the lighthouse steering memory safely to port pleasure: the sun. I see in imagination myself looking around my old room, seeing the various lithographs depicting Jewish moments in time.

If I am like an Israelite, whom his God has liberated: if I, having new-secured freedom, shall forget my once having been enslaved, I'll continue to be enslaved; but now escaped have I. Was I sent only to wander in this wasteland, now east, to Eden, like Cain? What did I kill, ignorance? Getting lost in the west, to alien worlds; somewhere in the south, the wind striking me; in the north, a solitary meditation the womb within which I die.

I think about not thinking; I had been free once to see the sky, bathe under the sun, unburdened and unbounded, so that I could at length speak my mind, without fear of either unjust retribution or malicious iniquity: this time–a fickle flame–has passed, never to be rekindled again. How would the heart in its variant logics, in an otherwise imprisoning mockery, know of this experience, the expulsion of which has been forgotten, not known but even once?

Left for us in our wanderings, are questions cradling questions? Would they not be, then, in like light to loss? Being nearly self-same, it would then be hammered further by this bountiful-sultry sun into the pale moonlight of idolatrous regret. The sweat of my brow *is* insignificance, especially when compared to the sweat of my thoughts.

I think about my writings, the keys to unlocking many doors, but I have yet to be shown which doors go with which keys. Knowledge is denied to me, kept away in the dark; it is lost to the solitary wounds of nature, none of which may be healed, but heeded. Were I able to apprehend their message, I would then begin to rejoice fervently, only to awake–either by necessity or time–to reality's more celebrated dream. Awakening thus is cruelly much in like manner, I imagined, to an imprisoned slave, who is reawakened only after sampling, but drunkenly, the intoxication of being free in his dreams, which is not freedom. It's delightful and delectable dimensions that, with their enchantments, beguile the bellicose truth! Now the awakened slave is returned to consciousness only to find himself in the end: where he had begun, in a comic, cosmological succession of folly. He would, perhaps, after much tribulation and instruction in the poetry of the cry, come to realize, gradually understand, that he was locked up in a cage within in a cage, within which remains wombed yet another; it would be a savage disenchantment, a detestable degree of degradation.

I cannot politely excuse myself from myself, at least not yet. Upon inspection, two letters have been written in my emotion; I saw one that was addressed to my desires, and the other to my fears. Time is the fire in which the choice burns to be realised. Handing me the letters, grief informed me that the letter's appearance has not yet been lost to time. It could not hold onto silence, but it shall; I'll have to wait for a better tomorrow. And this emotional letter writing was to its foundation, my entire existential apparatus.

I saw the sky canvassed with numerous shades. Its painter dips the brush of a cloud into the stroke of various movements. This comes across my skin as wind, tickling my touch. The eastern wind sweeps against the leaves. Further to the north, I observe a flock of migrating birds. Their numbers were graceful in both form and format. I walked slowly, but my awareness was nestled deep in my motions. A thought wrinkled through them, as wind across the surface of the sea. Spying earthlier things, I hear the rustling of leaves. I catch the note of a robin in its singing; its music echoing throughout the background. Now quiet. I judge where I was against whatever I had been near by their pitch, and its reception to my ears. Ahead of me are sand, greeneries, and the falling of a leaf; it falls lazily before me, as if to ask me to be its school playmate, not wanting to go back to silence or loneliness, especially now since it has been separated from its relations, relations that are high above, no longer reachable. Taking up seat by some empty little lot in front of the beach, where possibly a previous house might have stood, I began to think back on certain events. Their effect was posed in vigour. I found myself wanting to pace in a diagonal fashion across my mind, but refused. I took a folded letter from out of my pocket; it was old and written to an older warm acquaintance:

To Daniel:

P.R.C.N.N. To reawaken memory is to reinvent one's reality.

There is, so I would expect, a certain substantial sentiment while, though inhabiting the sphere of misunderstanding, is not so general and by no means the label with which to name particular interest, which is, again, a general misperception as to how, and why I am attempting to contact you, Danny. Of all the questions that I yet have heard, it seems to me most strange that the unexpected, being a necessary agency, does but come when it is least expected to come. The question, however, might be more important than the answer. Answers change. Surely, you have not forgotten this potent pattern that history affords us. It is as common as it is to breathe. Then again, it is less common than common in a '*by common*' by common commonality. Were we to receive some answers, then, perhaps, so would the questions change.

I shall only write of the question here. Remember this.

If, only for clarity, you are finding in these words substantial ambiguity, insidious phrasing and little in the way of explanation, then I write truly that the simplicity of the matter is thus: The difficulty lies in framing the questions rather than in finding the answers; this is most true when engaging in empirical investigations. Know that it's not the question that's the answer's shadow, but rather the answer's the painting, the question the frame, which holds it together.

With these words, as it aught to be hither writ, the rebellious nature of my being is by expectation an accordant reply, which has, I suspect, to climax in authenticity when the vulgar unwritten and the vernacular silences have presented themselves. As such, note you well this: these words from a distant time in the general purpose of this questionable existence are in the end existent solely to express the inmost and that which by nature belongs to the being of all our People.

In our last contact there was a rather sharp reticence in my words, as well as in our actions, collectively. As it regards my communicability, its sphere, it was most disagreeable; and this is again in the sphere of scrutinized judgement. Still, what is worse is that I myself never saw your face outside the confines of the school, in actual fact we never remembered anything regarding our interactions outside the unnatural limits, borders and imaginary edges of the school.

On a related note, as I must here confide in you, such an institution has never been more aptly named perhaps than a high school, a place where strangely enough most of its student body is indeed high, though I suspect not on education. This usually holds true with its staff and faculty. I ever so wonder what it is if not education? Pardon this, my meandering indiscretion.

What I am writing about is that time as well as chance has given me ample opportunity to take care of some unfinished business in the area. And yes, you yourself Danny made my list. If you receive this letter and receive it well, perhaps contact is possible once more. I would have preferred to phone you personally but since the date of your arrival is undetermined to me, the next best chance would be one of the following: (I) Telephone me at my number.

The moment you do contact me by means of the telephone, my answer-phone shall say to leave a message after the tone (don't be discouraged) here I am; just say my name and I'll answer (we shall take it together from there, I imagine).

One way or the other, you have my word that I shall keep in touch. Friendship, I believe, and I think you will agree with me, is something that shouldn't be lost to time, distance or a general difference of degree. It is with such logic that forms the architecture of this my letter to you.

P.S. How have you been? Your father tells me you have been away on vacation, quite the klug. Your understanding the letter, I trust, is less important than your contacting me. Oh, by the way, those initials at the beginning of the letter mean: Please Read Carefully Neologistic Note.

Danny, unfortunately, never contacted me again.

There's some broken glass laying on the street nearby, reflecting puddles that are in turn quite reflective themselves. I saw my reflection through the fractured mirror, my awareness of my awareness proving pivotal. I am a refugee, not seeking refuge. I am Sephardic, olive-skinned, and my Israeli birth but a haphazard reality, to which I only reply that it was a choice–which not being a choice–was itself made in absence to its concept as choice. I'm not particularly tall, but affording the contrary impression, my dark complexion uncannily agreed with my lighter tendencies to discourse, to mediate on all matters Jewish.

My hair, which was most like my father's, is an appropriate cut for an ordered mind, in a chaotic world: black and thin, it conducted the wild of the winds with faithful resistance, which gave it the appearance of being somewhat untidy, but by no means unruly or distasteful, let alone crude. My eyes, these being most like my mother's, were interestingly reminiscent of healthy tree bark, reflecting the light accordingly.

I recall how my grandmother described my great grandfather. In her journal she wrote:

In the art of argument, one could describe his motions, especially in reference to his hands, as being reflective of the world, but they were not, actually. They are reflective of a part of the world, the sea namely. For once he is given over to his swift or serious discourse, his hands adopted movements which could only be described upon observation as uncannily reminiscent of the waves, which, crawling toward land, are soon sucked backed into the abyss. The nature of his hands is like motions following themselves as they make their way towards the shore. Thin in shape and attractive in form, he is inescapably Jewish, and is inevitably European, regardless of the accidental birth. Yes, that it is thus, there can be no doubt at all about that.

I was fond of labelling such journal entries as "Nostalgia and the Loss of Time", or "Overture of Silence (Heaven and Its Stars)".

Near the surf, I found in hearing the waves, how a simple beauty was presented. When one wave comes ashore, a memory is sucked back into the vast mind from which it came; but when a wave is swallowed back into the ocean, likewise a memory is washed on shore, a beached relic for which consciousness may interpret itself. It is as if reflecting on the old school, a means by which I hear a moving hand proclaim, "I require the spectators to believe what I, the Director, am implying that they believe."

Before the first day of school, I wrote about some observations and reflections that I had made during the course of my walking to school this morning:

Witnessing how heaven has been starred, I see how they are honoured and haunted by the overture that pursues it, which gives nature presentation. It's the hour of hunting, which is the awareness of the audience itself.

Once the overture is lost, the eye like a camera retracts to reveal naked reality, which assumes the form of the Western Wall in Jerusalem. The impression is distant and dictates we are in the presence of an insidious reflection of the celestial candles. What casts their projection is water, and it is this image, which introduced by means of the eye and less than the ear, that ultimately impresses upon the audience perpetuity, a sense of eternity.

A petty pond–so it seems–keeps prisoner a whole host of creation in the reflection.

The screen is dripping a body of belief as to whether or not we are indeed being lead to believe that we are presently seeing the surface waters in reflection to the heavenly scenery; which having graced the screen with what was once thought to be inflexible-structural integrity: it now unfolds to genuine intrigue, dissolves. Without time's oppression, the waters are disturbed. They begin to disfigure that which can only be described as a graceful disturbance of silence and stillness; this is done simultaneously. Being reminiscent of shattered glass, the choreography has to be incandescent, but smooth. The camera pulls inward; the image becomes as it has always already been.

This is what we see: a Jewish worshipper. His facial expression must secure the impression that it is absent from either disgust or hatred, so that he is undisturbed somehow when we find him gently removing remaining fragments birthed by vandalism, which by another name is called ignorance. This speaks, I suspect, to the presence of a black testament, which may be in actual fact timeless. It is an unnatural hope, perhaps.

The camera pulls back once more, and reveals a child. The Jewish worshipper was thus being seen not by our eyes, but by his own, and his through the lenses of his eye spectacles. Suddenly, without distractive sense or disturbed logic, the hateful crime is mirrored. We were always already in a mirror image.

Wind. The seen reverberates like surface water undulating, causally scaring the sea's face with celestial starring. Only now is the actual scene seen. The ocean. Focus gently.

The spectatorship sees the stars, but the projection of colour and texture remains thus controlled! The stars are captured in a map.

Enter a classroom.

This classroom does not speak to any particular age; its general atmosphere is Western European. The chalkboard is clean, the desks neither in wait nor use. The mood is mute and anonymous, a monotonous morning melancholy.

No students, or teachers; it is simply pervaded by a potent emptiness, like the synagogue.

Gradually, very gradually, like the rusting away of precious metals, a student enters the classroom. His face is hidden. Only his shadow is captured by glimpse. The heavenly map is found, and by means of little mirroring we are drawn to the fact that the student came, somewhat nonchalantly, in search for it. Having found his map, he now has no further purpose in being there, and so it is that he leaves the classroom, and is thereby returned to primitive emptiness.

Dawn. The sun is awoken–as if by habit–to chase away the dream, so as to cause the natural landscape to flourish in a sea of renewal and distant jubilation.

Enter a mutual music, old quiet violin, in part rather than whole, hence first twenty-five to twenty-six seconds, approximately.

A child emerges from the door. He is walking to school, most likely. There are other children walking to school, too; pedestrians are present, as is common with the working day in any urban environment. The scene is as strangely welcoming as was the first. The portrayal of time is ever of the slightest touch of quieter motions: violent stillness.

The colours most dominant are a sober predawn-like blue with an English green and red. Autumn. There are leaves being blown in the wind. Trees grace the alleyways. This is a distant keenness of the absence of passerbys now. The school itself comes into sight.

My mind was not in concert with harmony, as it ought to have been. My mind had become a rope, which was being pulled at both ends by the things that were all too apparent. These extremities equally exerted force, thus propelling my nausea. This is how I sensed my state, for while I thought the hopeful within myself: it would be—so I discovered—a perpetual power in my perceptions having only beginnings, not ends. I thought it stationary, as it would have been in the nature of a rope.

When to my lungs the soft late afternoon breezes came to cease their quest, as dose a ship when anchored and asleep at port, I could not bear time. For yet I lived while lost within a maze, a tortuous solitude from which stillness had sprung; I the lone survivor did survive; but now to know in a little sleep of nature's reasons, as to why so contrived of a place made me to eternally weep, is of poor validity and little repose. Uncertainty is its kingdom; so now on lonelier shores am I free to contemplate the unmovable.

An old abandoned lighthouse.

The winds had been blowing softly and the sea was whispering gently, making the surrounding vegetation appear either keenly awake or asleep; I couldn't register which.

Then, suddenly, I heard glass breaking. Judging from where I was standing, I raised my head to see the top of the tower, and there saw a student extending his arm, readying his whole body for the throw; and with a natural posture of inclination, threw another bottle into the distance, the echo carrying the fracture well passed the place of impact.

Walking to my right, feet in the sand, I now stood myself at the front, my head lifted, I began looking directly now at the student whom I had now begun to fully recognize. How curious, it was Heschel, the student who spared me much grief in the locker room.

"Is there a problem?" the student atop the tower called back down to me.

Raising my voice, the light in my face, I called back to him, "Minus the glasses, and I'll have twenty-two hundred vision; but besides that, no."

"Do I know you?" he asked, leaning to see me better, his voice clearly indicating how gently bemused he was becoming.

"No, not exactly; we met at school today but we weren't properly introduced. My name's Akeiden; do you mind if I come up there?"

"Do as you please," he said, posturing as if to indicate his nonchalance.

Continuing to look at him directly, refusing to resign myself from speaking with him, I answered, "Okay, I think I will." And having said this, I heard some species of snake hiss from the distance, somewhere in the vegetation.

Climbing the stairs, how little did we know what nature had in store for us. The strange thing is that, even if we could know in advance what was about to happen, we would have found in our own way of looking at things a solution to allow what had happened to happen; a part of such wholeness. This is humour, God's sense of it at least;

and what's the big boss's sense of sticking it in, simple, really. Violent irony. I was about to make a friend—

Part III
Afterword

The Seven Commandments of Angstrographical Filmmaking

1. *Disiconoclastacy* is the presence of angst. This, in turn, is what happens when the untagonist (the protagonist and/or antagonist, be him prime or not) does not discriminate between two elements of a most uncertain propensity in nature. In the first place it is a desire unfathomably philanthropic—which now has only begun to become indistinguishable from infinitely torturing necessity, to change the world. They cannot have this particular quality removed from their character, though with the mind haunted by longing, any divergent action results in a cause for sickness to argue in their stomachs, be it a melancholy meandering thought, a certain disrespectful distress in sufferance, a need disjointed, disengaged occupation, want or woe as digression for disassociation, coldly distant interest, or disagreeing industry. Still, it is alien to them and it frightens them into frustration from all once found to be familiar, that it becomes foreign, fanciful; fantastically fictitious. Their conscious willingness to have prayer answered, together held in respect by a virtuous nature, a subtle tenacity as chief instrument, this being a natural forcefulness in speech made most royal with a martial-like temperament from joint-efforts in instruction and meditation, that it awakens them to how they've been awoken, so that it too wakes in them the want to wake others to what they've been awakened to. The presence of angst is, therefore, the creation of an emotional cocoon from which the main character(s), after suffering an almost countless variety of certain events, all of which are ironic in their

violence, emerge fundamentally transformed. This development, though, leads to a maturity wholly removed from the province of disingenuous designs, to a partial degree, then, which is a tolerance for false things, especially when their content concerns correspondences, to be observed all where nature has her accustomed dominion, thus making for them whole in order to make what seemed wholly fragmented simply whole again. This theme of a mind made whole, though, is not estranged from that which is to be found most dangerous in nature, for with the greatest of desires there awaits, too, the worse of disappointments, thus with the work for redemption diseased, ill-made now by forces of a most incorruptible corruption, the effect to after-times is set and the outcome inevitable. The angstrographical piece is, then, a detailed and disturbing history of that disiconoclastacy.

2. Messianic Extremecy: The belief in redemption requires patience, this itself being privilege impressed upon the pilgrim by open prayer and observant piety. The objective serenity with which a word is uttered betrays an unheard lamentation, and though he of religion and virtue is far from being a stranger to sorrow, be it of his own or, add or subtract as is required of necessity, of all over which Lord God has dominion; the prevention of paradox is indulgent, though with cause for contradiction a life to be cut-short and immediately. The eye there be with which to see does observe evil; the ear for silence to hear hears lamentation as substitute, with the voice of God–be it now called conscience, a cry almost fabled calling forth for faith from fear feeding faithlessness that accustomed frenzied feast, which is food for fuelling feelings of a general disillusionment in the design of virtue, the immediate removal of which casts the world weak, wretched, wrong—a vicious instrument of unadulterated debauchery, a part of the playing field where it's better to stay away from, about which say not a word to anyone at all at any time, itself, then, a vice. With purpose deprived, and the design for goodness diseased, it seems certain almost that there's this time to come, of a sacred strangeness decreed by nature and necessity, when forces subservient shall either subscribe to or be succumbed by a redemptive agency and/or agent, from whom there is no depriving. This privilege of patience, about which piety decrees and to which all prayers prayed from pious pilgrim lips go, is a face of the fundamental in fortifying faith for those whose minds have been burned with Promethean fire, and, speaking of whom, cannot have either removed or resolved the immortal imprint that lingers conscience deep within them. Given their terrible task to bear, which God-Given be, the privilege, which of back alley beggars and enthroned tyrant kings is alike born, is denied them, and with it destroyed, an exile and a wanderer, the untagonist is told to take it upon his or herself to redeem the human condition, let not patience be an excuse for inaction and intelligent procrastination, and with violent testimony taken account, is unable to wait for that redemption, being now not alone the means by which to achieve it but the mind through which it thinks, the body through which it receives what sense there is to bring, and that self-same voice and arm through which to pray with action now. Messianic Extremecy, then, with a partial respect now held, is the license by which the chief character(s) has the right not to wait for God, becoming in effect his own Messiah.

3. Solicicence: The untagonist is not necessarily isolated by a violent history. Violence is established with irony, be it, too, a thing of ubiquity as made most demonstrable in human depravity, and may mean anything from the death of tender parents to a terribly lonely day at school; the face of it is held in common but, being experienced disproportionately, does find signature in each soul and thus an individual audience for each theatre. It's, also, worth to wait the end for me to say that the social situations of the piece are not defined by blood so much as they are defined by loneliness, longing and lamentation.

4. Occultastrophe: The angstrographical piece is incapable of being classified cultic or any other like genre, as, for example, thriller, gothic, horror, *etc. Any* violation of this commandment invalidates immediately the work in question from being labelled angstrographical.

5. Ucarnacity: What haunts the agency in the angstrographical is humanitarian, not hedonistic; and nor are the confused, carnacious and coincidental in anyway significant in the creation of subject matter. That is not to say, however, that they whom the ancients in the conquered lands called "Delight" and "Aphrodite" may not play some part in the minor characters, or, indeed, be used as a source material, a rich Mediterranean soil to have certain seeds sown, in order to produce such effects as comic relief, or the conflict the Dove Goddess creates in everyday situations because of her misunderstanding, mainly when she's caught up in a net in the act by that lame blacksmith.

6. *Inprincilency*: To each untagonist there is revealed what may be fully understood nowadays as a worldview, with the supporting and remaining characters in possession of what is tentatively referred to as a world peephole.

7. *The Agisony*: For a large class of cases, though certainly not for all, the central characters are usually from age thirteen to age thirty-nine.

The Seven Commandments of Angstrographical Writing

1. The first commandment remains in effect, touching every corner of the work.

2. Messianic Extremecy is accompanied by Parallelism, which is when irony and paradox overlap, either by desire or design, to create chaos in the character.

3. The third commandment remains in effect.

4. The fourth commandment remains in effect, the literary equivalents being what they are.

5. The fifth commandment remains in effect.

6. The sixth commandment remains in effect.

7. The Divine Proportion is to be imprinted into the angstrographical work.

Concluding Remark

Of the angstrographical one may truly observe that its one principal purpose—if any there were—is in the quieting of the storm, to be returned to silence, and with its subject matter destroyed, to become obsolete.

TATE PUBLISHING, LLC

127 East Trade Center Terrace
Mustang, Oklahoma 73064

(888) 361 - 9473

TATE PUBLISHING, LLC
www.tatepublishing.com